NOT OF NATURAL CAUSES

"You want to know if it's necessary to call for the sheriff, I think you should take a closer look and decide for yourself. I want you to see his throat."

Mr. Tyson moved closer and peered down at the dead man's neck, then raised his eyebrows. "Is that—I assumed he had died of natural causes, but that looks like—"

"A piece of cord. Von Baulmer certainly did not die of natural causes, Mr. Tyson. He was murdered!"

Don't miss any of the lusty, hard-riding action in the new Charter Western series, THE GUNSMITH:

And coming next month:

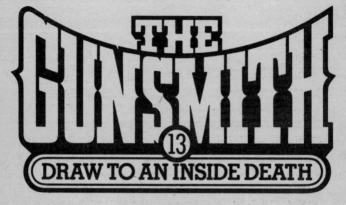

THE GUNSMITH

13

DRAW TO AN INSIDE DEATH

J. R. ROBERTS

ACE CHARTER BOOKS, NEW YORK

THE GUNSMITH #13: DRAW TO AN INSIDE DEATH

An Ace Charter Original

Published by arrangement with the author

ISBN: 0-441-30868-6

First Ace Charter Printing: February 1983

Published simultaneously in Canada

Manufactured in the United States of America

Ace Books, 200 Madison Avenue, New York, New York 10016

To CHRISTOPHER ROBERT RANDISI,
because he's a pistol

Prologue
Two Queens, Nevada

"Did you get the list?" the taller man asked as the shorter man entered his office.

"Of course I got it. I'm the one who has to send the invitations out."

"Let me see it," the tall man said. When the shorter man handed it over, the tall man read it, and then frowned. "I don't like this."

"What?"

"This name," the tall man said. "I know who this guy Clint Adams is. They call him the Gunsmith. What's he doing on the list? He's no gambler."

"I didn't ask him why he invited who he invited," the shorter man replied. "Maybe he figures to get a thrill by sitting at the same poker table with a gunman."

"Maybe. But I still don't like it."

"Don't worry about it. He can be handled." The smaller man hopped into a chair and went on, "Let's have a drink on it, before I send the invitations."

The taller man opened a drawer in his desk and

1

took out a bottle of whiskey, but he was still staring at the list, shaking his head.

Taking the bottle and opening it, the other man said, "Come on, stop letting it bother you."

"Maybe we could leave his name off the list."

"That would arouse suspicion. Look, let me do the worrying, all right? Have a drink." He took a swig from the bottle and passed it back.

Taking the bottle, the taller man said, "I don't know. I've just got a feeling that Adams is gonna fuck this whole thing up for us."

"No chance. No chance in hell."

ONE

The invitation to the biggest poker game of the year came as a complete surprise to me. I was the reluctant owner of a reputation or two, but being a top poker player was not one of them. To say the least, the invitation made me very curious and also eager to accept. I found myself excited at the prospect of sitting down to a table of the finest poker players in the world and testing myself against them. I did think of myself as a good poker player, but it remained to be seen if I would be able to hold my own with them.

Of course, all of that means that I accepted the invitation and went to Two Queens, Nevada.

Two Queens, Nevada is a town built on and around poker. The man who built it was the one who had been holding these annual high-stakes, by-invitation-only poker games for the past ten years. This was, in fact, the Tenth Annual Two Queens Poker Game. It was not, however, just a game, it was a contest that had been known to go on for days; one year it had gone on for two weeks before one man had actually come out the only winner. It was sort of like a duel to the death, and only one winner was allowed, no matter how long it took.

The founder's name was Peter Tyson. Ten years ago he had attended a high-stakes poker game which had been held in a small house on that very spot, and he had used his winnings to build Two Queens, Nevada. Every time he won—and he had won six of the past nine games—he sunk more of the money into the town. He had named the town after the final hand with which he had won the first contest—a pair of queens.

By now Two Queens was an impressive sight for a town barely ten years old. All it needed to become a major city was a railroad.

As I rode into town I saw that there were several hotels and saloons to choose from, and there were *two* banks. The saloons had names like The Busted Flush and The Fourth Deuce; the hotels were The Two Queens Hotel and The Ace High Hotel. Even the banks were called The Bank of Two Queens and The Royal Flush Bank.

I drove my rig up to the livery—that had no name—and turned it over to the liveryman to put up. I gave him instructions on how to handle Duke, and saw that he was sufficiently impressed with the big fella to follow them.

With my saddlebags and rifle in hand I tried to decide what my first priority was, a room or a drink. I decided on the room; this way if I got involved with a couple of beers I wouldn't have to break off in order to get a room.

I picked the Two Queens Hotel, which was the largest and looked to be the oldest. Go for experience, I always say.

"Could I get a room, please?" I asked the clerk, a snappily dressed young man in his early twenties.

"Certainly, sir," he said, reversing the registration book so that it faced me. "May I ask your name, sir?"

"Adams," I said. "Clint Adams."

"Ah, Mr. Adams," he said, immediately recognizing the name. I was used to that, but then I found that my rep had nothing to do with his familiarity with my name. He grabbed the book before I had a chance to sign it and said, "Mr. Tyson has made arrangements for you to stay at his home. I'm to send him a message when you arrive."

I frowned and said, "Just me?"

"No, sir. He's made the same arrangements for everyone involved with the game."

"I see."

"You can leave your things with me, sir. Transportation to the house will be here shortly. Several other members of the game have arrived as well."

"I see," I said again.

He stared at me expectantly, and then said, "Uh, your things, sir?"

"That's all right," I told him. "I'll hang on to them. I'll be over at the saloon, washing down some trail dust. Can you send someone over there when the transportation arrives?"

Eyeing my saddlebags as if they might have had gold in them, he said, "Certainly, sir. My pleasure."

"Thank you," I said. I picked up my rifle and my saddlebags and headed back for the saloon. Aside from a change of clothing, I also had my little .22 New Line in my saddlebags, and I didn't want to leave it in anyone else's hands.

I went to The Busted Flush Saloon and ordered a beer. Drinking it with my back to the bar, I took in the impressive layout before me.

It was early, yet at four of the six house poker tables there were games in full swing. There were a few tables available for pick-up games, but they were empty. Aside from that, there were faro and blackjack tables available, and a roulette wheel. Poker was the main game, however.

"Nice set up," I commented to the bartender.

"We like it," he said, with a bland, bored look on his face.

"Who's the owner?"

He stared at me for a moment, then said, "Mr. Tyson."

"That figures."

"Who are you?" he asked boldly.

"My name's Adams. Clint Adams."

His eyebrows went up and he exclaimed, "You're the Gunsmith!"

I winced and said, "Not so loud, friend."

"Oh, sorry," he said, covering his mouth with one hand. All of a sudden the bland look faded from his face, and he actually looked friendly. He appeared to be in his early thirties and was very slim and dark.

"You should have told me who you were as soon as you came in," he scolded me. "Your drinks are on the house."

"If that's the case," I said, "let me have another cold beer."

"Sure, Mr. Adams."

He drew me a second beer and set it down in front of me.

"Some of the other players have arrived in town, also," the bartender offered.

"Is that so?"

"Yeah. Look over there, at table three."

Assuming that the tables numbered left to right, I picked out table three. There were five players and the dealer.

"The guy in the dark suit, the one who *looks* like a gambler?"

I spotted the man he was talking about. Dark suit, white broadcloth shirt, string tie and black, flat-brim hat with a silver band.

"I see him," I said, and I knew who he was before the bartender could tell me. "Monte Blake."

"Monte—" he started, then stopped short when he realized what I'd said. "Oh, you know him?"

"No, but I've heard of him," I said. Blake had played in this game three times before, and had won it once. It looked like he was back for another try.

"I guess he's warming up, huh?" the barkeep asked.

"I suppose so," I said. I turned to face him and gave him a second opportunity to impress me. "Who else is in town?"

His face brightened, and he said, "Well, they're not in here right now, but I heard that Deke Talon was here, and some dude named Barnaby."

I'd heard of both men. Deke Talon was a gambler who worked most parts of the West. Barnaby was a well-known figure in the Barbary Coast, and he claimed that he'd played in all the biggest games in England and France.

"Anyone else?"

"Not that I heard."

"Okay, thanks."

I picked up my beer and started to circulate. Tables two, three, four and six were in use; I worked my way around to table three and stood there watching Monte Blake work.

And work he did. This was his job, and he played with more concentration than anyone I'd ever seen. His hands were immaculate and performed their tasks of dealing and shuffling with speed and grace. I thought perhaps that my watching might annoy him, but he didn't even notice me—or if he did, he didn't let it show, and he didn't let it affect his game.

He was on a hot streak, and took eight of the ten hands I watched, no matter what the game was. Draw, stud, it was all the same to him.

I was almost finished with my beer when I felt someone tap me on the elbow. I turned and had to look down to make eye contact with the little man.

"Transportation is here," he said.

"Little man" was not an exaggeration. He couldn't have been more than three and a half feet tall, and he'd tapped me on the elbow because he couldn't have reached any higher without standing on a chair.

"Excuse me?" I said.

"Your ride is here," he said. "You're Adams, right?"

"That's right."

"There's a buggy outside waiting for you and the others. The only man I have to find now is—"

"Monte Blake," Blake said from behind us. He'd collected his winnings and stood up, and had been listening to our conversation.

"Are you Blake?" the little man asked.

"That's right."

"Then we're ready to go."

"I suppose so," I said. "But what's your name?"

"I'm Rollo. Follow me."

Rollo waddled towards the door on his short legs, and Blake and I followed. I couldn't tell whether he was a midget or a dwarf, because I didn't know the difference, but his head was too large for his body, and his hands were also very large.

"Adams?" Blake asked me as we followed. This was the first chance I'd had to get a good look at him. He was about my age, with dark hair and gray eyes. He was still clutching a deck of cards in his left hand.

"That's right," I said.

He extended his hand; I took it and shook it shortly.

"I've heard of you, but I didn't know that poker was one of your areas of expertise."

"Neither did I," I told him, "until I received the invitation."

He looked at me to see if I was kidding, but before he could ask we reached our buggy, which looked like an expensive stagecoach, with a driver up top. Little Rollo told us, "Get in and we can get going. Sinclair?"

At this the driver reached down, Rollo took hold of his extended hand with both of his, and Sinclair lifted him up and deposited the smaller man next to him.

From that vantage point Rollo looked down at us and said, "Hurry, hurry."

"I guess we'd better hurry," Blake said, and opened the door. I let him get in first and then followed and pulled the door shut. Two men were already seated on one side, so we took the opposite seat, facing the rear. I reached up and pounded on the roof to indicate that we were ready to go.

During the ride we introduced ourselves. Deke Talon did not look like a gambler, he looked like a brawler. His hands were large and gnarly, and he had a big bulbous nose that had been broken once or twice. Still, his reputation as a poker player was unchallenged. He acknowledged the introductions wordlessly, simply nodding his head.

Barnaby was the dandy I had always heard he was. The only other man I knew who dressed nearly as well—on certain days—was Bat Masterson, but Bat was barely into his twenties, and Barnaby had to be in his late forties, early fifties, although he appeared to be in marvelous shape for a man that age. He was very nearly a legend among gamblers, and I was looking forward to playing at the same table with him.

"I must admit I'm not surprised to find these other gentlemen here," he said, "but your presence does surprise me somewhat, Mr. Adams. I don't believe I've heard of you."

"We must travel in different circles, Mr. Barnaby."

"Oh, just Barnaby, please. That's what everyone calls me."

"I've heard of Mr. Adams," Blake spoke up, "but it's his prowess with guns that I know him for, not with cards."

"Guns?" Barnaby asked.

"Some people have been known to refer to him as the Gunsmith," Blake said. Barnaby accepted that piece of information without a change in expression, but it was Deke Talon's reaction that surprised me. His eyes went wide, and he actually stared— or gasped—at me for a few seconds before recovering his composure and staring out the window.

Why did my name have such an effect on him? I wondered.

"As I told Mr. Blake, Barnaby," I said, ignoring Talon for the moment, "my invitation is more of a surprise to me than anyone else."

"Indeed?" Barnaby asked, looking surprised. "Well, I suppose we'll have to leave the explanations up to our host, won't we?"

"If we're due any," I said, and left it at that.

TWO

Conversation was rather stilted during the ride, and Blake tried to get up a little four-hand draw poker game, but there were no takers. He continued to fiddle with the deck in his hands, and I wondered idly what would happen if I reached over and took it away from him.

"I know you've been here before, Mr. Blake," I said, breaking a long silence.

"Monte, please," Blake said. "Yes, three times."

"What about you other gentlemen?"

Deke Talon looked at me and gave a short shake of his head, and then Barnaby said, "I suppose I always managed to be elsewhere in the past. This is my first time."

I wondered if this was the first time he'd been invited, but with his reputation I doubted that very much.

"Anybody know who else has been invited?" I asked.

"We won't know that until we get there," Blake answered. "The invitations are never publicized."

"We'll just have to contain our curiosity a little longer then," Barnaby said.

When the coach finally stopped, the door was opened from the outside by the man called Sinclair. Now that I was seeing him up close and with his feet on the ground, I could see that Sinclair was as unusual in his way as his little friend Rollo. This man was at least seven and a half feet tall, with a face that looked as if it had been chiseled out of granite.

"All out," he said in a bass voice, and he stepped aside to let us out while he held the door.

When the four of us had left the coach, Rollo called to us from the steps and said, "This way."

The house was immense. It was two stories and probably had as many as twenty rooms or more.

"Come on, come on," Rollo said impatiently, shifting his weight from one short leg to the other as he waited for us at the head of the stairs.

"Look at this place," Blake said, holding his deck of cards in both hands.

"Right out of jolly old England," Barnaby said. "It looks like a palace."

Deke Talon was still not talking, and I caught him giving me sideways glances from time to time. Something about me bothered him, and to tell the truth, he was starting to bother me as well, and not just because he was staring at me. I was starting to think that I'd seen him somewhere before, but I couldn't think where.

Could he have been bothered by the same thought?

I brought up the rear as we ascended the steps, just an old habit of not having anyone at my back if I could help it. Rollo opened the front door with a key and we followed him in.

The foyer was huge and we stood before a large staircase that widened as it came down. Walking down the stairs now was a tall man with a neatly trimmed brush mustache, dark hair touched with silver at the temples, and a broad smile on his dark, handsome face.

"Gentlemen, welcome," he said. As he reached the bottom of the stairs he extended his hand and shook hands with each of us in turn.

"I am your host, Peter Tyson."

We took turns identifying ourselves, and he nodded and said, "My pleasure," after the last introduction was made.

"I could have guessed who you all were," he said, proudly, "but no matter. I am very happy to meet you all—except for you, Mr. Blake. We have played against each other before."

"And I've enjoyed it each time," Blake assured him.

"As have I." He turned to Barnaby and said, "An honor, sir, to finally have you here. This is far from your first invitation."

"I'm happy that I was finally in a position to accept," Barnaby said.

He looked at us all, still with a beaming smile, and then said, "Joseph will show you all to your rooms, and we will have dinner promptly at seven, through there." He pointed to a doorway on our right which I presumed led to the dining room.

"Have the others arrived?" Blake asked.

"Three of them have. We are awaiting the remaining two players."

"Will we be starting tonight?" Barnaby asked.

"Oh, my, no," Tyson answered. "We will have dinner and then we will go to the drawing room to get acquainted. The first round of play will begin tomorrow evening."

Blake riffled the deck that he held in his hands, which I took to be a show of displeasure. He obviously wanted to get started as soon as possible.

"Joseph," Tyson said quietly. At that point we all became aware of the man who was standing behind us. Now, this one was normal, and rather ordinary looking at that. About five-eight and forty years old or so, he was remarkably unremarkable in appearance, with no outstanding features whatsoever.

"If you gentlemen will follow me, please," he said, starting for the steps.

"I will see you all at dinner, then. There are baths available in all of your rooms for your pleasure."

"You're very thorough," Barnaby said, "and very kind."

"Nonsense," Tyson said. "I want you all to be as comfortable as possible...when I take all of your money."

Barnaby laughed while Blake grinned, but Talon and I were too busy exchanging surreptitious glances again to react.

"Please," Joseph said, and we proceeded to follow him upstairs.

It was only then that I noticed that Rollo had disappeared.

"You will all be in the west wing of the house," Joseph told us. "Except for the lady."

"Lady?" Blake asked.

"There is going to be a lady in this game?" Barnaby asked. "How wonderful."

"I don't like playing against women," Talon spoke up, startling us all.

"My God, he speaks," Barnaby said, and Talon gave him a scowl and lapsed into silence again.

Talon was shown to his room first, followed by Barnaby, me and then Blake. Our rooms were on the same side of the hall, one after the other.

"It is four o'clock now," Joseph said. "Dinner is at seven . . . promptly."

"Thank you, Joseph," I said, and he shut the door and took Blake to his room.

I dropped my saddlebags on the bed and set my rifle down, marveling at the dimensions and furnishings of the room. I had never seen a hotel suite that size and had been in many houses that were smaller. Off to the right was a separate room with a bath, and the water had already been heated for me.

"Well," I said to myself, starting to undress, "I've got three hours to kill, I might as well start now."

I shucked my clothes and got into the hot bath. The water eased the aches that traveling had put into my bones, and before I knew it I was falling asleep. I woke up some time later and the water was tepid. I got out of the bath, still feeling drowsy, dried myself off and crawled naked under the covers of the most comfortable bed I'd ever been in.

THREE

I woke up with a start and checked the clock that rested on the night table next to the bed. It was six-ten. I had enough time to dress and make dinner at seven. It was my first night in the house and I didn't want to get Joseph peeved at me. He had made a special point of the word *promptly*.

I got up, washed my face to wake myself up, then got dressed, wishing I had some clothes that would do my surroundings justice. Since I didn't, I stopped worrying about it and worried about something else: my gun, and whether or not to wear it while in the house.

My reputation dictated that I rarely—if ever—go without my gun, but I couldn't help feeling funny about wearing it to dinner, let alone to the game when it started. At least with the game there could be an excuse. Tempers had been known to flare at a poker table, but what about a dinner table?

I decided not to allow myself to be intimidated by my surroundings, and I strapped on my gun. Better to be on the safe side. Besides, there was the uncomfortable feeling I was getting from Talon. Sooner or later one of us was going to remember the circumstances under which we had met before, and the gun might just come in handy at that point.

Fully dressed, I left my room and started down the hall. As I came out of the west wing and made a left to walk to the stairway, I saw someone coming from the east wing and caught my breath.

That we had a "lady" in the game had been an understatement. The woman walking towards me was breathtaking. Tall and regal, with a lot of dark hair that was piled on top of her head, she wore a gown that was cut low over full, rounded breasts, and the green of her dress was reflected in her eyes.

As we spotted each other we both stopped walking and I felt terribly self-conscious about the way I was dressed. I wasn't even wearing a jacket, and she looked as if she were going to a presidential ball.

"Hello," she said, smiling. Her voice was rather heavy and low, but it sent chills running up and down my back. Her neck was long and smooth, her bare shoulders creamy white.

"Hello," I replied, forcing the word out.

"Are we going to the same place?" she asked.

"Dinner," I said, again only able to manage a single word.

"Then why don't we walk together?"

"My pleasure," I said, proud of the fact that I'd been able to double my previous output of words. I approached her and extended my arm, and she linked hers through mine. We started down the steps together and she said, "Who are you?"

"Clint Adams."

"My name is Diana Caine."

"Pleased to meet you...*Miss* Caine?"

She smiled and said, "Yes, it's *miss,* but if we are going to play poker against each other, I think you had better call me Diana."

"My pleasure," I said. "And you must call me Clint."

"Is this your first time?" she asked. I stared at her and she said, "At the game."

"Oh, yes," I said, realizing what she meant. "This was my first invitation. How about you?"

"I was invited last year, but I was unable to attend," she explained. "I'm happy to be able to make it this year."

We reached the main floor and made a right to walk towards the door Tyson had indicated earlier.

"Do you know where you're going?" she asked.

"Have faith," I said, and she smiled.

"You seem to be a very capable man," she said. "I'm in your hands."

I walked into the dining room with Diana Caine on my arm, and I could see in the eyes of the men seated there that they envied me.

Tyson rose from the head of the table and said, "Ah, dear lady. The last to arrive. I see you've found yourself an escort."

"Yes, we bumped into each other upstairs, and he was kind enough to bring me here," she said, disengaging her arm from mine so that she could give her hand to her host.

"Allow me to see you to your seat, dear lady," Tyson said, and I watched as he walked off with her and ushered her to a seat next to him—not that I blamed him.

Once he had deposited her in her seat he approached me again and said, "Mr. Adams, a moment of your time, please, in private?"

"Of course."

He took me aside, out of earshot of the others at the·table and said, "Ah, about your weapon, Mr. Adams."

"What about it?"

"Ah, it really isn't necessary for you to wear it in the house, you know."

"Mr. Tyson," I said, patiently, "I have the misfortune of having a reputation with my gun, and because of that, I am forced to keep my gun with me wherever I am. If it offends you in any way, I will be happy to leave your house—"

"No, no," he said, hastily. "I won't have that. If your gun is a condition of your presence, then so be it. Please, take your place at the dinner table and we will start our meal."

"Thank you, for understanding," I said.

"Not at all. I'm sure it must be a burden to you."

We walked to the table and took our seats. Probably by virtue of being the last male to arrive I ended up at the foot of the table while Tyson and Diana Caine were at the head. She was sitting to his left, while Barnaby was seated to his right.

Over dinner informal introductions were made, and I found out who the other four players were.

There was Pop Walen, who had been a gambler for more than forty years, and apparently was still going strong. He had a shock of white hair with eyebrows to match and a heavily lined face. As ancient as he appeared to be, however, I noticed that his hands were rock steady.

Directly across from me was a man I had never heard of, and with good reason. His name was Klaus Von Baulmer, and he had come from Germany to play in this poker game. He was a large man with very short gray hair and what appeared to be a fencing scar across his right cheek.

Another of the remaining players was European, a Frenchman name Henri—which he pronounced *On-ree*—Pleshette, a small, dapper man with a hairline mustache he apparently took great pride in. He kept taking long looks down the table at Diana Caine, but if she noticed she didn't let on.

The last man was Daniel Rose. He was a traveling gambler who didn't care where he had to go to get into a big game. He was probably the youngest man in the tournament, not yet thirty, and it was a tribute to his ability that he had been invited.

Dinner was comprised of pheasant, several well-prepared vegetable dishes, salad and an excellent wine—and, of course, the first course, which was a French soup which Pleshette assured us was delicious.

"My chef will be pleased that you like it, M'sieu Pleshette," Tyson said, obviously pleased.

After dinner Tyson rose, put his arm out to Diana Caine, and asked the rest of us if we would follow him into the drawing room for after-dinner drinks and a discussion of the rules governing the game.

We were able to request whatever we wished to drink, and I decided against asking for a beer and went for a brandy instead. Once we were all set with the drinks of our choice, Tyson began to discuss the rules.

"Some of you have been here before, so you will

please bear with me as I go over the rules for the first-timers. It's very simple, gentlemen—and lady. We are here to play poker, pure and simple. That means stud or draw, and that is all. No wild games, please. We are not children here, we are professionals."

Suddenly I felt as if everyone was looking at me, wondering what I was doing there, and I couldn't really blame them. *I* was wondering what the hell I was doing there.

He droned on about the normal rules of poker applying and covered every possible argument that could come up during the game, so that no questions would ever arise while the game was going on.

"Does everyone understand?"

"Oui," the Frenchman spoke up. "I believe we all understand zee rules, M'sieu Tyson, but when do we play?"

"Patience, my friend. The rest of the evening belongs to you. You may stay here and get acquainted, go to your rooms, or go to town if you wish, but the game will not start until tomorrow evening. If any of you are so eager to play I will provide you with transportation to and from town, or you may make use of the table in the poker room and have a small game of your own tonight."

"I'm for a game," Blake said, holding up his ever-present deck of cards. "Anyone game?"

He laughed at his own joke, and he got four or five players to sit down with him. Barnaby begged off, saying he would wait for the big money, and Diana Caine said she would be going to her room to get some rest from her trip.

"I think I'll do the same," I said, in spite of the fact that I had already slept.

Tyson himself disappeared to some private part of the house.

Diana Caine threw a glance my way as she left the room and I was sure she was sending me a message, the same message she had been sending my way all through dinner.

Smoke signals, using the smoke that was coming from a fire inside of her.

I watched as she left the room—as did the others—and then as they filed into the poker room to play, Barnaby and I left as-well.

"A lovely woman," he commented.

"Beautiful," I agreed.

When we reached the main foyer she had already disappeared from sight.

"Going to your room?" he asked me.

"Yes. I think a rest is a good idea."

"Well, I'm going to take a walk outside and then do the same. Good evening. See you in the morning."

"Good evening, Barnaby."

I waited until he had left and then started up the stairs. When I reached the top I stopped. Should I go to my room and wait for her to come to me, or should I go looking for her room?

She didn't know which room I was in, but as far as I knew, she was the only guest staying in the east wing.

I decided to go looking for her. If I was wrong about her signals then she could always slap my face and send me packing.

If I was right, however, then it was a good thing I had gotten some rest when I did. She didn't look like the type of woman who liked to spend her time with a man sleeping. . . .

FOUR

Finding her room was no major problem because she had left her door ajar.

I approached her door and knocked softly.

"Come in," her low, well-modulated voice called out.

I pushed the door open and saw her standing by the door, wearing a dressing gown that made it plain there was nothing underneath it. It molded itself to her large breasts and wide hips.

"Close the door."

I closed the door and turned to face her, marveling at the fact that there was not a hint of tension in the room. It was as if we had both done this countless times before with each other.

"I was afraid you didn't get my message," she said.

"Oh, I got it, all right."

"Just in case you're still not sure . . ." She opened the dressing gown and allowed it to fall to her ankles.

Her body was flawless. Pale skin, glowing in the

light from the lamp, large well-rounded breasts with tawny brown, swollen nipples, and a large tangle of black hair between her legs. Her thighs and calves were perfect, and as she turned for my inspection I could see that the cheeks of her buttocks were high, smooth and firm. Her dark hair, no longer piled atop her head, hung past her shoulder blades, forming an ideal backdrop for her beautiful face.

Her eyes were wide-set and shaped like a cat's; her nose was strong and straight, her mouth wide and full-lipped. In fact, her upper lip was almost as full as the lower one, giving her mouth an even lusher look.

My first urge was to taste that mouth, so I approached her, took her by the shoulders and did so. Her mouth was willing and eager beneath mine, and her tongue crashed through the barrier of her lips into my mouth. It was sweet and insistent, as insistent as her hands, working feverishly at divesting me of my clothes.

"Please," she said against my mouth. Her hands had opened my pants and found what was inside, and as she grasped it tightly she said, "Please."

We tumbled to the bed together and I shifted about, removing the remaining clothes so that we could press our naked bodies together.

"Mmmm," she moaned into my mouth as my swollen penis rubbed against her furry thatch. She moaned even more as I moved my lips down her neck, over her shoulders and finally settled on first one nipple and then the other, sucking them to incredible hardness.

"Oh, Clint," she said, cradling my head in her hands, pressing my face tightly to her bosom.

I put one hand between her legs and began to stroke her, pet her, manipulate her. She thrust her hips up to meet the pressure of my fingers and my hand.

"Oh, my dear," she whispered. "I want it, I need it . . . now! Please!"

"Yes," I said, mounting her. "Now."

I slid into her easily and was suddenly surrounded by her warmth and her wetness. I began to move in deep strokes and her hands roamed over my back, finally settling on my buttocks, seeking to pull me even further inside of her.

"Oh, yes," she said with virtually every stroke, "yes, yes, yes . . ."

"Yes," I repeated, as I felt the tension in my legs, my building orgasm.

She came to hers first, writhing violently beneath me, trying not to scream, even though we were supposedly alone in the east wing.

"Oh, God, Clint," she gasped, with her eyes tightly shut, and then I exploded into her, filling her up as her muscles stroked me, almost sucking my seed from me.

She kissed me then, covering my mouth with those lush lips, driving her tongue deeply inside my mouth, and then simply licking my lips, wetting me with the sweet taste of her mouth.

"Message received," she said, smiling. I moved to pull my semi-erect penis from her, but she grabbed me and said, "No, stay awhile."

"Here?" I asked, moving my hips. "Or here?" I added, indicating the room with my eyes.

"Well," she answered, "if you stay here in my room with me, you would have to go back to yours in the early hours of the morning. I don't think it would do for our host to find us both in the same room, do you?"

"It might make for undue tension," I agreed.

"Well, then," she said, "why don't you stay awhile . . . here"—wiggling her hips—"and here"—indicating the room, and then, grabbing my face in her hands—"and here."

She pulled me down so that her mouth could swallow mine, and my penis was *semi*-erect no more.

FIVE

As we both agreed was wise, I went back to my room in the early hours of the morning, unde-tected—unless the little man Rollo was lurking about unseen.

It would be daylight soon, so instead of crawling into my own bed I took a tepid bath, deciding against calling for heated water so early in the morning. Afterward I dressed and left my room to go for a walk on the grounds.

I had slept very little that night, but it had been exhilarating, to say the least, and I was not tired.

As I descended the steps to the foyer, I saw Rollo come from a room to my left. Both the dining room and the drawing room had been to the right, so I didn't know what rooms were on the other side of the house. Possibily his own bedroom.

"Good morning," I said.

He had to look up the steps to see me, and he did so with a scowl on his face. I think he resented having to look up to the whole world in general, and he might have taken having to look even farther

up, to the stairs, as a further insult to his size—or
lack of it.

He stared at me for a long moment without reply,
and then continued on across the foyer, as if I did
not exist. I continued descending the steps, and then
watched him as he disappeared from sight through
the doorway to the dining room, an unfortunate man
who probably was justified in having a cynical dis-
position—not to mention a nasty one.

Outside it was cold, but Nevada could not match
Montana in that department. The short time I had
spent there, very near the Canadian border, had
shown me what true cold really is. From that time
on, Southwestern winters no longer seemed something to dread.

It was no longer truly winter, as spring was on
the horizon. It was, however, still a bit brisk, and
if I *had* been tired, I would not have been any
longer, following my walk.

The walk around the house took me some time,
and I was even more impressed as I approached the
front again. I saw a man walking my way from the
opposite direction, and recognized him as our host,
Peter Tyson.

"Good morning, Mr. Adams," he greeted.

"Good morning, Mr. Tyson."

"A brisk morning walk, eh?" he asked. "To re-
vitalize you after a long...night?"

I frowned at him, wondering if he knew where
I had spent the night in spite of my precautions.

"I just felt the urge to walk," I said.

"Ah, well, I walk, too, every morning," he said.
"It wakes you up, makes you know you're alive."

I nodded my agreement, and he turned to walk

back to the front of the house with me.

"Were you comfortable last night?"

It was an innocent enough question, so why did I think there was a hidden meaning in it somewhere?

"Comfortable enough."

"Is there anything we can do to make your stay more comfortable?"

"There is something, yes," I said. It was something that had occurred to me during my bath. "My horse. If I'm going to be out here more than a few days, I'd like to go back to town and bring my horse out."

"Well, I'll save you the trip," he said. "I'll send someone to get him."

"I'm afraid that wouldn't be possible, Mr. Tyson."

"Why not?"

"Duke is a one-man horse. He wouldn't allow anyone else to ride him. I'd rather go back and get him myself."

"All right. After breakfast I'll have Sinclair take you back to town. He can come back without you, and you can return when you're ready. Just make sure you're back by eight, for the game, or by six, which is when we'll have dinner today."

"Thank you, Mr. Tyson."

"No problem," he said. "I want your mind to be free of any problems when you sit down at that card table."

"So do I," I agreed, thinking of Deke Talon. Talon had been in the back of my mind since last night. I was sure I had seen him somewhere before, but I didn't want to have to keep wondering about it while we played poker. There might be something

I could do in town about trying to identify him to myself.

Breakfast was not the group meal that dinner had been. Rather, as the players came down they were served, and since I was one of the first, I was ready to leave before Diana had even come down from her room—which was probably all to the good. A woman has a way of looking at a man she's spent the night with that's a dead giveaway.

"I'm ready to leave," I informed Tyson after I'd finished my meal.

"I'll have Sinclair out front in ten minutes," he said. He signaled Joseph, who came and received instructions to that effect.

"Thank you," I said, after Joseph had gone to inform Sinclair.

I went out front to wait for the big man to bring a buggy or carriage around. When he showed, it was in an open buggy, smaller than the coach we had first come in.

He stopped it and then simply sat there, without looking at me or speaking to me.

"Good morning, Sinclair," I said, getting into the buggy. I didn't expect an answer, and I wasn't disappointed. He started the lone horse up, and we were off.

I kept going over Deke Talon's face in my mind during the ride, but Diana Caine's face kept forcing its way into my thoughts.

When we reached town I stepped down from the buggy and turned to tell Sinclair he could go back, but no sooner had both of my feet touched the ground, than he had the horse in motion and was heading back to the ranch.

"Thanks," I said to his retreating back.

I turned and sought out the telegraph office. When I found it I stepped inside, and then started to wonder who I could send a telegram to.

I was friends with quite a few lawmen around the country, so I decided to send off telegrams with Talon's description to some of them and see if it meant anything to them.

That done, I told the clerk where he could find me to bring any answers that should come, and then I headed for the livery. On the way there I passed the sheriff's office and decided to stop in and announce myself.

"Sheriff?" I asked the man behind the desk.

He lowered the posters he had been reading, and I could see the sheriff's star on his chest. He was a thin man, tall I saw as he rose, with a hawk nose and sunken cheeks. His age was hard to gauge, just as easily forty as fifty.

"I'm the sheriff. What can I do for you?"

"My name is Adams, Clint Adams."

The sheriff frowned and said, "I know that name." He began leafing through the wanted posters on the desk.

"You might know the name, Sheriff, but you won't find it, or my likeness, on any posters."

"Where then?"

I shrugged and said, "Possibily on the right side of the law."

"Adams," he said. "Clint Adams. I've got it! Sure, you're the one they call the Gunsmith."

"Unfortunately."

"You were a lawman for a while, weren't you?"

"For a long time."

"You still wearing a badge?"

I indicated my chest, where there was no badge, and said, "No, not for a long time."

He regarded me for a long moment, then sat back down and said, "Well, what can I do for you?"

"Nothing in particular," I said. "I usually let the sheriff know when I come into a town. It's always easier than having him hear it some other way."

"Sounds like a good idea. Where are you staying?"

"At Tyson's ranch."

"You playing in that game?"

"Yes."

"Well, good luck. I wouldn't mind seeing an ex-lawman take all those gamblers for what they're worth."

"I'm going to give it my best shot," I said. "There is one thing you could do while I'm here, though."

"What's that?"

"Are those posters up-to-date?" I asked, indicating the sheaves of paper covering his desk.

"They sure are," he said. "I've just been going over them myself."

"Would you mind if I took a look through them?"

"Help yourself," he said. As I came forward and began to do so, he asked, "Looking for anyone in particular?"

I looked up at him and said, "Just trying to fit a name to a face I've seen recently."

He waited a few moments until I'd given up and then said, "Did you find him?"

"No," I said, putting the posters down. "But then I didn't really expect to. Thanks, Sheriff—"

"Fulton, Tom Fulton."

"Sheriff Fulton. Thanks, again."

"Sure, my pleasure," he said. "Give them hell at that game."

"I'll do my best."

I left the sheriff's office and went straight to the livery.

"Come for your horse?" the liveryman asked.

"That's right."

"Right handsome animal."

"Thanks. I'll saddle him myself, thanks."

I paid what I owed and went to Duke's stall.

"Hiya, big fella," I said. "How are you doing?"

He shook his massive head and I patted his nose and told him he was coming with me now. He seemed to appreciate the fact and showed impatience as I saddled him.

Mounting up I said, "Okay, Duke, boy, let's get a move on."

I decided not to stay in town any longer than possible, and we started back to Tyson's ranch immediately. I had paid attention to the route on the way in, having ridden in a closed carriage the previous day.

Duke wanted to stretch his legs, but I wasn't in a hurry to get back, so we compromised. I let him gallop about a hundred yards, and from then on we just took a leisurely ride.

Having Duke on the ranch would take one problem off my mind, but there was still Talon. It wouldn't have bothered me so much if it hadn't been for his reaction to *me*. It seemed that whatever memory he had of me was not a pleasant one, and for all I knew, he *did* remember where we'd last met.

And that might end up posing a serious problem.

SIX

When I rode up to the front gate of Tyson's ranch, I noticed for the first time his brand prominently displayed above it. The brand was, predictably, a double *Q* for two queens.

As I rode up to the front door Tyson was coming out, and he waved to me.

"Back so soon?"

"There was nothing to keep me in town," I said, shrugging. "Where can I put my horse up?"

He ignored the question and did a slow turn around Duke, admiring him.

"That is quite an animal," he said.

"I know."

"I don't think I've ever seen one like him."

"There couldn't be one."

"How much would you take for him?"

"Nothing."

"I could make you a generous offer."

"There are two reasons that wouldn't work, Mr. Tyson," I told him. "One is that I could no sooner sell Duke than I could my right arm, and second, you wouldn't be able to ride him anyway. He's a one-man horse."

"Is that a fact?"

"You wouldn't want to find out for yourself."

He examined Duke a little longer, then looked at me and said, "Take him to the stable out back. You must have seen it this morning, during your walk."

I had caught a glimpse of it. It was set pretty far away from the house.

"Lunch will be at one," he advised me. "Some of the others have a game going in the poker room."

"No thanks," I said. "I'll wait for the real thing."

"My sentiments exactly."

He turned to go back in the house, and I rode Duke around to the back, where we found the stable.

"Holy cow," I heard a voice exclaim as I dismounted. I turned in the direction of the voice and found myself facing Diana Caine.

"Well, hello."

She came walking out of the stable leading a bay mare, but she only had eyes for Duke at that moment.

"He's beautiful," she said. "May I touch him?"

"You could try," I said. "He'll let you know if he doesn't like it."

She approached him, and as she reached a hand for his nose I put my hand on his neck. He jerked his nose from her once, but when she tried again he allowed her to pet him. I patted his neck at the same time, just to be on the safe side.

"My God, he has such an aura of . . . raw power. I'll bet he's the fastest thing on four feet."

"I haven't found anything faster."

She turned her head towards me and said, "I was just going for a ride. Care to join me?"

"Sure," I said. Duke had not even broken out in a sweat on our ride from town, and I knew he wouldn't mind carrying me a little while longer—for a good cause.

"Could I ride him?" she asked, with her eyes shining.

"I'm afraid it wouldn't be advisable to try," I said. "Nobody but me has ever ridden him, and we both like to keep it that way."

"I can understand that," she assured me. She rubbed his nose once more, then walked to her mare and mounted up easily.

I climbed on Duke's back and said to her, "I see you know your way around horses."

"I love them," she explained. "Grew up around them."

"Which way do you want to go?"

"Mr. Tyson said I should ride behind the stable and not towards town. He said it was prettier."

"I won't notice," I said. "I've got something else to look at."

She smiled demurely, and then wheeled the bay around and started off.

"Come on, Duke," I said, giving him a little kick, and we followed her.

We rode for a good portion of what was left of the morning, just talking. I did a lot of talking without saying much, but I'd made an art out of that. I also recognized it when someone else was doing the same.

So did she.

"Have you noticed how much we've been talking

without saying anything?" she asked at one point. "I still don't know anything about you except that you were born in the East."

"And I don't know anything about you except that you were brought up around horses," I said, "and sit one better than most men I know."

"Well, thank you, sir," she said. "But there are some other things we know about each other."

We were standing side by side next to a tree and she leaned over to be kissed. I met her halfway, and her mouth opened beneath mine, sweeter than fresh fruit.

"Clint..." she began as we broke the kiss, and her eyes said the rest. I watched as she dismounted, tied off the bay and then walked over beneath that big tree. She unbuttoned her blouse and peeled it off, and then I dismounted and went over to help her. First we got her clothes off, and then mine, and then we were going at it beneath that tree, rolling around on the soft grass. We finally stopped rolling with me on top and I drove myself deep into her. There was no give to the earth, like there is with a mattress, and I penetrated to her core, causing her to gasp and buck beneath me. She put her legs up around me, held me tight and matched my thrusts with her own.

Out of breath, we dressed again, smiling at each other and looking around to see if anyone had come up on us while we were...busy.

"We'd better get back for lunch," she suggested, untying the reins of her bay from the branch she'd secured it to.

Duke sensed it was time to go and came walking over to me. Diana mounted up, and as I took Duke's reins I caught him looking at me.

"Don't be giving me the eye," I muttered to him. "Just because you been gelded doesn't mean I can't have any fun."

SEVEN

After dinner we drew lots to see where we'd be sitting. With ten players the only game you'd be able to play would be five-card stud, so we were to split up into two tables, until such time as there were only enough players left to make up one.

My table included Barnaby, Pop Walen, Henri Pleshette and Monte Blake. Table two was Tyson, Diana, Von Baulmer, Daniel Rose and Deke Talon.

I was glad not to have Talon at my table for now. I'd be able to concentrate on my game without distraction.

The same went for Diana.

The buy-in price of this game was the invitation. We could walk in with ten dollars or ten thousand dollars. I had considerably more than ten, but considerably less than ten thousand. I was also sure that I had a lot less than any of the other players. Still, I had been invited and I wanted to play, so I'd scraped up what I could without leaving myself totally broke, and here I was, about to play in the biggest game of my life.

"We are all aware of the rules," Tyson said as we sat down. "Good luck to everyone."

And the game began.

The first deal fell to me by virtue of high card, and I called seven-card stud.

I folded when none of my first four cards matched, and the hand went to Pleshette. He had a third deuce in the hole to beat the two pair held by Pop Walen and Monte Blake. Barnaby had dropped out on the sixth card when the others had started raising.

The opening bet had been fifty dollars, but that would go up as the game went on.

The way the tables were set up, table one—Tyson's table—was between us and the door. I sat with my back to the wall, as always, and from my seat I could see everyone at the first table, and the door. As the deal passed to Barnaby, who sat on my left, I looked over and saw Diana raking in the pot from the first hand.

There were no chips in this game, just paper money. That way you could feel your money as it came and went.

Rollo was constantly in the room, taking care of anyone who wanted a drink. Some of the players were drinking whiskey, some beer—like me—and some, like Barnaby, didn't drink at all.

"A clear mind and a steady hand," he said, shaking his head at me as I ordered the beer.

"I can't even play right unless I'm half drunk," Monte Blake spoke up, grinning.

Everyone had their own rules. I just liked to have a glass of beer on the table in case I got thirsty. Every so often I'd ask for a fresh one, even if the one I had was still half full. When I did take a drink I wanted it to be cold.

The deal went around the table twice before I took a hand. I'd had a couple of decent hands, but had gotten beat by better ones, and I had folded early in almost half.

At the end of three hours, I was down a thousand dollars, and Tyson called for a break.

"Let's let the room air out, what do you say, gentlemen—and lady?"

"I'm for that," Monte Blake said, even though much of the smoke in the room had come from his cigars.

He couldn't take all of the blame, though. With the exceptions of Barnaby, Tyson, Diana and myself, everyone was smoking one thing or another.

I stood up during the break to stretch my muscles and watched as little Rollo opened a couple of windows in the room, letting the smoke filter out.

There was a bar set up at the far end of the room, and now big Sinclair—big and *ugly*—came into the room and stood behind the bar.

Out of curiosity, I approached Tyson and said, "Excuse me, Mr. Tyson."

"Yes, Mr. Adams?"

"Since this game is no secret, may I ask what kind of security you have against a hold-up?"

"A hold-up? Here?" he asked, laughing. "There has never even been an attempt, Mr. Adams."

"That doesn't mean there won't ever be one."

"Quite right." He pointed to Sinclair and said, "Sinclair is outside the door as long as play is going on. Rollo is inside. They are both armed. I also have four men constantly circling the house while the game is in progress."

"Very thorough."

"Thank you. How has your luck been?"

"I don't know," I answered. "I'm either winning or losing."

It took a moment before he realized I was joking, and he smiled and said, "Quite," and walked to the bar to talk to Diana, who had been getting a glass of brandy, the first drink she'd taken all evening.

Diana had taken pity on us men and had not worn a low-cut gown. However, the dress she was wearing molded itself to her so thoroughly that you could plainly see the lovely shape of each breast. During the break, she was the center of attention, but once the game started up again, we were all business.

From time to time I caught her looking over at me, which I didn't mind, but damned if I didn't catch Talon looking my way every so often, and that bothered the hell out of me.

As we started play again, I took the first two hands with fairly moderate cards, then caught a flush and lost to a higher one. That's the way the cards were.

Play went on into the early morning, with two more breaks, and by the time we were ready to call it a night, things had evened out pretty much. I was down five hundred, and I don't think anyone at the table was up even half that.

It seemed to be a different story at the other table, though. From the way Daniel Rose was acting, he was losing a bundle. Being younger and less experienced than the others, he was not able to hide his emotions—while winning or losing—as well as the other players were.

Rose was complaining about his bad luck as some of the players had an early morning nightcap before turning in, but no one else wanted to discuss the first round of play.

"Jesus," he was saying, almost literally crying into his beer. "Four of a kind! How do you lose with four of a kind!"

"To a bigger four of a kind," Monte Blake said. We all said amen to that and went to bed.

It only took one glance between Diana and myself to establish that we both preferred to go to our own rooms and get some sleep after the long poker session.

When I got to my room I dropped onto the bed while still fully dressed and went over my play in my mind. All in all, I hadn't done too badly. Down twenty-five hundred at one point, I had come back up two thousand, and that wasn't bad. I didn't know for sure who the winners were, but I suspected that Barnaby was not only ahead, but that he was the class of the table. A few hands had come down to the two of us in the end, and I had taken only one of those. At least I hadn't folded or allowed myself to be bluffed.

Not too bad, I remembered thinking, and then I was asleep. . . .

I was awakened by an insistent knocking on my door and staggered from the bed to answer it.

"Yeah, yeah . . ." I muttered as I approached it. I felt as if I had only been asleep for a few minutes.

When I opened the door I found my host, Peter

Tyson, standing there with a worried frown on his face.

"Mr. Tyson," I said, puzzled.

"Yes, uh, Mr. Adams, I'm sorry to, uh, have to wake you up so soon—" he stammered, obviously very upset about something.

"Well, no, that's all right," I said, trying to focus my eyes. "What time is it?"

"It's, uh, only about nine o'clock," he answered, which meant that I had been asleep for about four hours.

I rubbed my eyes vigorously and said, "Is there a problem, Mr. Tyson?"

"Uh, well, yes, there is very definitely a problem," he answered, rubbing his hands together.

"What is it?"

He chewed his lip awhile and then said, "I come to you with this, Mr. Adams, because of your reputation and because you were at one time an officer of the law. You will no doubt know how to handle the situation much better than I—"

"Just what is the situation, Mr. Tyson?" I asked, getting very impatient now.

"Uh, perhaps I'd better show you," he offered.

"Now?" I asked. I was still wearing the same clothes I had worn at the game, and I also wanted to wash up.

"Oh, yes, it must be now."

"All right," I said. I picked up my gunbelt, strapped it on and then said, "Lead the way."

"We don't have far to go," he said. I followed him down the hall and he stopped three doors from mine.

"Whose room is this?" I asked.

"Von Baulmer's."

He reached for the doorknob and pushed the door open. When he didn't go in I brushed by him and saw what was making him so edgy.

The German, Von Baulmer, was lying on his back in bed, and his face was a mottled bluish color. There was a length of cord wrapped around his throat, and he was dead.

EIGHT

I moved toward him and could barely make out the cord because of the way the flesh of his throat was swollen over it.

"Who found him?" I asked.

"Joseph," he answered. "He came to me, but I didn't know what to do...and then I remembered you."

"And my reputation."

"Yes....Is he dead?"

"Oh, he's dead, all right," I assured him.

"You haven't touched him—"

"And I don't intend to," I said. "Besides, I've seen enough dead men to know. That's not exactly the healthiest complexion I've ever seen."

"What should we do, then?"

"Do?" I asked, turning to face him. "There's only one thing we can do, Mr. Tyson. Send someone for the sheriff."

"The sheriff? Is that really necessary? It will alarm the other guests—"

I frowned at him, and then wondered how close

a look at the body he'd taken before calling me.

"Did you look closely at him, Mr. Tyson?"

"I—uh—" he said, nervously.

"Did you even come into the room?" I prodded.

"Ah, well, Joseph...did, but I merely—I saw the color of his—his face—" He broke off when I raised my hand and beckoned him into the room. "You want me to come in?"

"Yes," I answered. "You want to know if it's really necessary to call for the sheriff, I think you should take a closer look and decide for yourself."

"Uh, ah, well, very well," he said, and took several hesitant steps into the room. He was annoying the hell out of me with his behavior, which was not at all in keeping with what I had seen of him up until that point.

"Closer, Mr. Tyson," I said. "I want you to see his throat."

"Very well," he said. He took several bolder steps and was then standing next to me. "What am I looking for?"

"Look at his neck."

He peered down at the dead man's neck and then raised his eyebrows.

"Is that—I assumed he had died of natural causes, but that looks like—"

"A piece of cord, yes," I said. "Von Baulmer certainly did not die of natural causes, Mr. Tyson. He was murdered."

"Murdered!" Tyson said, shocked, recoiling from the word. "In my house? This is terrible."

"You see now why the sheriff must be notified," I said.

"Yes, of course," he said, backing away from

the bed. "I will have Sinclair go to town at once."

He hurried to the door and I called out to stop him.

"Tyson."

"Yes?" he said, not turning to face me until he was one step out of the room, into the hall.

"Don't let anyone else know about this until it's absolutely necessary."

"Of course not."

"And I'll just stay here until the sheriff arrives, to make sure no one touches the body."

"Yes, yes," he said. "Although I don't know who would want to."

He hurried off to send for Sheriff Fulton, and I shut the door behind him.

I wasn't worried about who would want to touch him now that he was dead, but about who had killed him . . . and why.

NINE

Fulton arrived almost an hour later, which was pretty good time, considering Sinclair was not built for speed.

As the door opened I got up from my chair and greeted the lawman as he entered the room. Tyson stayed behind, a respectable distance from the corpse.

"Adams," Fulton said, by way of greeting. "What have we got here?"

"I think you can see that pretty clearly," I said, indicating the man on the bed. "He's been strangled."

"Well, I wish that big . . . jerk that came for me had told me that," he said, annoyed.

"What did Sinclair tell you?"

"Only that Mr. Tyson wanted me out here as fast as possible. I could have brought the undertaker out here with me, as well, with his cart."

"I can supply you with a wagon and driver to take the—uh—body back to town, Sheriff," Tyson said from the door.

Fulton looked at me first, then at Tyson and said, "That's very kind of you, Mr. Tyson."

"Sheriff, don't you think we'd better have the door closed while we discuss this?" I asked Fulton, giving him the eye.

"Yeah, that sounds like a good idea," he agreed. "You don't mind, do you, Mr. Tyson?"

"Oh, not at all," Tyson said. "I will see to my guests' breakfast."

He pulled the door shut and Fulton and I were alone with the dead German.

"What's the story here, Adams?"

"I don't know any more than you do, Sheriff," I assured him. "Tyson woke me up this morning, nervous and tense, and brought me here."

"Why you?"

"He said that because of my reputation he thought I would better know how to handle the situation."

"And you told him to call for me?"

"Right."

"Well," he said, digging in his ear with the pinky of his left hand, "I sure ain't used to having people do the right thing when something like this happens. I appreciate it."

I nodded and he walked around the bed, examining the body from every angle.

"Any idea?" he asked, bending over the body to get a closer look at the neck.

"About who killed him?" I asked. "I've been thinking about it, but I haven't come up with any answers yet."

"Well," he said, standing straight up with his hands on his hips, "I don't mind telling you that I ain't used to dealing much with murder. I'm a town sheriff, not a damned Pinkerton detective." He turned to me and said, "I guess I could use some help."

"Sheriff, I'm here to play cards."

"That's so," he agreed, "but if I stop the game, you won't be playing cards no more."

My initial reaction was that he was bluffing. He wouldn't dare try to close down a game that was being run by the man who built the town. On second thought, if he was a decent sheriff, he was within his rights to stop the game, since a murder had been committed in the house—if he wanted to test his power.

"Sheriff, you stop this game and you're going to have an awful hard time keeping all of your suspects in one place."

"That's so, too," he agreed. "That's so."

"All right, look," I said. "Let the game continue. Since I'm here, I'll keep my ears open, maybe ask a few questions, and see what I can come up with."

"Well, I'd appreciate that very much," he said.

"Besides, these people are gamblers, and gamblers don't talk easily to the law," I pointed out.

"I have to talk to them," he said, then looked at me and added, "Don't I?"

"Go through the motions, Sheriff," I suggested, putting a hand on his shoulder as we walked to the door. "Ask a few questions, but don't push."

"All right, but you'll stay in touch with me, let me know what you find out."

"If I find out anything, you'll be the first to know, I promise. Why don't we get Tyson to lend you a couple of his men to carry the body down to a wagon, and you can take him back to town."

"Suits me."

"I'll talk to Tyson, you talk to some of the guests. A few of them may be done with breakfast about now."

"Maybe I should talk to some of them before they eat," he suggested, and as I stared at his poker face I realized that he had been joking.

If he had *tried* to make a bad joke, he couldn't have done any better.

TEN

By the time Fulton finished talking to a few of the guests, the others knew what was going on because they watched as two of Tyson's hands carried Von Baulmer's body down to the buckboard.

"What's going to happen to the game now?" Barnaby asked aloud as the men loaded the body onto the buckboard.

"The game will continue," Tyson informed him and any others who were near enough to hear. "Of course, if any of you want to leave—"

"Well, I'm not leaving, that much is for sure," Monte Blake said. "It would take more than this to make me give up a chance at the money that's floating around this game."

"Speaking of money," Pop Walen wondered aloud, "what happens to the German's?"

"We should throw it back into the game, somehow," Blake said, looking around for someone to back up his suggestion.

"I'm afraid that wouldn't be possible," Sheriff Fulton said. No one had seen him come out of the house, but he had heard Blake's remark while coming down the steps. Diana Caine came through the door behind him, and I assumed he had been talking to her.

Fulton stopped a few steps from the bottom facing Blake, but when he spoke he spoke to all of us.

"All of that man's personal belongings will go with me to town and be kept in my office safe—and that includes whatever money he had."

"Sheriff, that isn't fair," Blake complained. "Von Baulmer was the big winner last night. I—we—have to have a chance to get our money back."

"Not in this case, mister," Fulton told him, staring him down with that expressionless face of his.

Blake compressed his lips in annoyance, but said nothing further.

"Mr. Tyson, I'll just go up to the room and collect the dead man's things, and then I'll be ready to go," Fulton told Tyson.

"As you wish, Sheriff. My man is ready," he said, indicating big Sinclair, who hadn't moved since he had arrived with the buckboard. Fulton went back into the house as one of the hands covered the dead man with a tarp.

Diana came down the steps right behind me and put one hand on my shoulder.

"How awful."

"Are you all right?"

"Oh, I'm fine. The poor man asked me some questions, trying to be a detective, I suppose. He really wasn't very good."

"He's just a town sheriff," I said, echoing the very words Fulton had used to me, "not a damned Pinkerton detective."

"Do you think the Pinkertons will be called into this?" she asked.

"Not unless Tyson hires them."

There was some tension in her voice when she asked that question, but I put it down to the situation. Her hand was still on my shoulder and I put mine over it.

"Have breakfast?" I asked.

"I couldn't eat," she answered. "Not after this."

"How about some coffee?" I hadn't had breakfast and had seen dead men before, so now that it was all over—for the moment—I was starting to feel hungry.

She used her other hand to pat my other shoulder and said, "I'll have some coffee and watch you eat. Come on."

We went up the steps together and into the dining room. Joseph was there and I asked him, "Can I still get some breakfast, Joseph?"

"Of course, sir."

"Just bring me whatever's left."

"And the lady, sir?"

I was about to tell him that the lady wasn't eating, but she said, "I'll just have some of this, Joseph."

"As you wish, ma'am."

"This is something," she said, as we sat at the table.

"What is?"

"This place. Servants, more rooms than you could go through in a week. All of that I might have expected—although I didn't—but murder? What's going on, anyway?"

"Damned if I know."

"You know a little more than the rest of us,

though, don't you?" she asked.

"Why do you say that?"

"I saw you this morning, going downstairs with Sheriff Fulton," she explained. "Want to tell me what's happening here?"

"I still don't know," I said. "Tyson came to get me when they found the body. He thought with my background that I should handle things."

"And?"

"And I told him to call the sheriff."

She gave me a crooked look and said, "I'd rather have you than him."

"Why, thanks," I said, giving her a knowing look.

She smiled and said, "There, too. Who found the body, by the way?"

I started to answer, and Joseph came in with a plate that was heaped with eggs and bacon, and a pot of coffee, all on a tray.

"Joseph," I said.

"Yes, sir?" he asked, setting the tray down on the table.

"Joseph, why don't you sit with us a minute?" I invited.

"That would be impossible, sir."

"I'd like to ask you a few questions."

"I am quite capable of answering while on my feet, sir," he informed me.

"Very well. I understand it was you who found Mr. Von Baulmer's body this morning."

"That is correct."

"What were you doing up at his room that early after last night's session?"

"Excuse me, sir," Joseph said politely, "but am

I to understand that you are investigating this matter?"

"Mr. Tyson has asked for my help," I said, which I thought would be the best way to get him to co-operate.

"Very well," he said, accepting my answer. "Mr. Von Baulmer made a specific request that I awaken him at eight forty-five this morning. I went to his room and when I received no answer to my knock I tried the door and found it unlocked. I went in and found him. I then went and informed Mr. Tyson."

"I see," I said. "All right, Joseph. Thank you."

"Not at all, sir. Enjoy your breakfast."

I looked down at the mound of scrambled eggs that was spotted with slices of bacon and then Diana's hands flashed in front of me and lifted the plate. "Let's split it in half," she said.

"I thought you weren't hungry," I accused as she scraped half of my breakfast onto another plate.

"I'm a woman," she said. "I'm allowed to change my mind."

ELEVEN

For the remainder of the day—except for lunch—everyone seemed to go his own way. Tyson had made an announcement after Sheriff Fulton left with the body that we had until game time to decide whether we wanted to stay or go.

Tyson puzzled me. Now that Fulton and the body were gone, he once again became the self-assured host. Could the man have been that unnerved by a dead body? A man who had built a town up from a pair of queens?

Having roped myself into helping Fulton, I spent the afternoon engaging several of the other players in conversations designed to let me know if any of them had had a grudge against Vol Baulmer.

As it turned out, of the men I spoke to—Monte Blake, Pop Waner, Barnaby and Henri Pleshette—Barnaby was predictably the only man to have played against him before. Predictably because, though Barnaby played mainly on the Barbary Coast, he had played in Europe and made a habit of playing in big games. He said that he had run across Von

Baulmer once or twice in Europe and at least once in San Francisco.

"He wasn't deliberately unlikable," he added, "but he had an attitude of superiority that grated on the nerves of some."

"Had he grated on anyone here that you know of?"

"Only the people at his table last night," he said.

"Why is that?"

"He was the big winner of their first round. Apparently their table was not as evenly matched as ours."

"Rose was pretty upset last night," I said, pensively.

"He's a bad loser. Why are you asking so many questions, Adams? Is the old lawman in you coming out?"

That was as good an answer as any, so I nodded and said, "I suppose it is. Sorry."

"Don't apologize," he said, pulling out a slim cigar and lighting it. He saw me staring and said, "Oh, I smoke, but not when I'm playing poker. I even drink, on occasion, but only the most excellent brandy."

That was a slur on Tyson's choice of brandy, because I hadn't seen him drink any last night.

"Have you see Talon?" I asked then. Talon seemed to be avoiding me; I hadn't seen any sign of him all day.

"No, I haven't," Barnaby answered. "What is it with you two, anyway. Are you in love?"

"Why?"

"I see the way you keep sneaking looks at each other."

"We know each other."

"From where?"

"I don't know," I said. "I've been trying to re-member ever since the first time I saw him. I think he knows though."

"That doesn't sound good."

"It's not," I said. We were standing behind the house, halfway between it and the stables, and now we began to walk towards the house again. "It puts me at a distinct disadvantage."

"I would say," he agreed. "I'd watch my back if I were you...but, then, I get the feeling you've made a lifetime avocation out of that."

"I have, but I've found no pleasure in it," I replied. "Not in any of it."

TWELVE

Everyone stayed—but, then, that's a gambler for you. The game is everything. What gambler wouldn't give his life for one big score?

Table two played with four players now: Tyson, Diana, Rose and Talon. When Talon walked in, it was the first time I had seen him all day. Not that I had missed him; I just hadn't liked not knowing where he was.

Play began, and after a few hours, Danny Rose left no doubt in anyone's mind that he was losing— badly. At my table, things progressed pretty much the same as they had the night before. Barnaby was winning, and everyone else was losing, but nobody was really getting hurt...yet. Still, with the four of us losing small, Barnaby was increasing his stake in a big way. It would help him later in outlasting the last couple of players—providing we kept losing, that is.

I, for one, did not.

I discovered something about myself and about the big gamblers that night. The only thing that had separated me from them, up until that night, was the fact that they had more money than I did, so were able to play for higher stakes.

They were not necessarily better players than I was. When I realized that, I started doing a whole lot better.

I was still outclassed by Barnaby, but the rest of them were just a bunch of card players.

Three-quarters of the way through the session, though, Pleshette got hot and stayed that way until the end. I was up a hundred, Barnaby was up nearly a thousand, but it was Pleshette who ended up the high man, and he was beaming.

"I need a drink," he said as we called it a night.

"You deserve one," Barnaby said.

Danny Rose was the first one to the bar, complaining again about losing, getting beat with winning hands. When Pleshette ordered a drink from Sinclair, Rose started talking to him, but he was talking to the wrong man. The Frenchman couldn't stop smiling and that bothered Rose even more.

Being even a hundred dollars up made me feel like having a beer before bed, so I went over to the bar too.

"What are you grinning at?" Rose was demanding of Pleshette.

"My dear sir," Pleshette told him, "you must learn to accept winning and losing with the same—"

"Ah!" Rose snapped, slamming his empty glass down on the bar and drawing a menacing look from Sinclair. "That's easy for you to say when you're winning, but I'll get my turn. You'll see!"

Rose stormed out, presumably to go up to his room.

Tyson came over and told Sinclair to pour him brandy.

"Our young Mr. Rose does not take losing too well, does he?" he asked.

Still grinning, Pleshette said, "I am afraid not." He put his empty glass down and said, "Good night, gentlemen."

"Good night," Tyson replied, and I just nodded.

"I'm afraid bad losers and happy winners don't mix," Tyson commented after Pleshette had gone.

"I'm afraid not."

"And what about you, Mr. Adams?" he asked. "Which one are you?"

"I'm holding my own thanks, Mr. Tyson."

"Good, good," he said, looking as if he had something else on his mind. "I don't think I properly thanked you for your assistance in the sordid matter of this morning."

"That's all right," I assured him, "I was glad to help."

"Joseph tells me that you were questioning him this morning," he commented then. "He told me that you said I had asked you for your help."

"That's right."

"As far as it goes, that is correct, I must admit," he said. "But have you now taken it upon yourself to investigate the matter?"

"Not really," I replied. "Just the old lawman in me coming out. It does that once in a while."

"I hope we can forget the incident and concentrate on playing poker."

"I didn't notice anyone who was too preoccupied to play tonight," I said.

"Nor did I, which pleased me a great deal." He finished his drink and put down the empty glass. "Well, I have some other matters to attend to before retiring, so I'll say good night."

"Good night, Mr. Tyson."

Diana was waiting off to the side, surrounded by a circle of admirers—Barnaby, Monte Blake and, proving that just because there's snow on the roof it doesn't mean you're dead, Pop Walen—and when she saw that I was free she excused herself and approached me, warming a snifter of brandy in her hands.

"How did you do?" she asked.

"Fine," I said, but I knew from the strained look on her face that wasn't the question she wanted to ask me.

"What's wrong?"

"I . . . really would rather not be alone tonight, Clint," she said. "I can't get that poor man out of my mind."

She shivered, and I put my hands on her upper arms.

"Go up to your room. As soon as everyone has retired, I'll come to you."

"Make it as fast as you can, all right? Please?"

"As soon as I can, I promise."

She looked at the glass in her hand and said, "I think I'll take this up with me."

"I'm sure it's all right. Go ahead, I'll see you in a short while."

"Very short," she said.

I watched her walk from the room, and I wasn't the only one. When she was gone Barnaby came over with an amused grin on his face.

"Quite a lady," he said.

"I agree."

"I think she likes you."

"Do you really?"

"Yes, I do."

"What about you?"

"What about me?" he replied.

"Are you interested?"

He sighed and said, "Clint, old boy, that's just something else I don't do when I'm playing poker."

"You don't do very much when you play poker, do you?"

"Not very much," he said. "Just win. Good night."

THIRTEEN

I didn't even bother to go up to my room myself. I simply waited until everyone had gone up to theirs. Sinclair was still in the room when I left, but he was cleaning up and would be a little longer. I felt that I would be able to make my way to Diana's room without being seen.

The door was ajar, as it had been that first night, and I simply walked in.

"Diana," I called, softly.

I could see the empty brandy snifter standing on the dresser, and her clothes were on the bed. Off to one side was a curtained doorway; if her room was the same as mine—and it certainly seemed to be—that would lead to the private bath. The curtain was drawn now, and I walked over to it and drew it aside.

She was in the tub and she gasped, turning her head towards me, eyes wide, throat constricted as if about to scream.

"It's only me," I assured her quickly.

"Oh," she said, closing her eyes and taking a

great, shuddering breath. "You just about scared the life out of me."

"I called out when I came in."

"I guess I didn't hear you," she said. "I thought a bath might relax me, and Mr. Tyson assured me that I could always have heated water, so here I am. I guess I got too relaxed and didn't hear you come in."

I took a good long look at her now, stretched out in that tub with only half of her full breasts above the water, and at that moment I was anything but relaxed.

"You certainly do look, um, relaxed," I said.

I was standing right next to the tub, near her head, and when she turned she was looking directly at my crotch, where I was at half mast but swiftly rising.

"You don't," she said. She pulled one hand from the water, dripping wet, and cupped it over me, soaking my pants. "Oops," she said, with a sly look. "Now you'll have to take off those wet pants and get into the tub with me."

"I don't think it's big enough," I said.

"We can fit," she assured me, stroking me through my pants.

"I have a better idea," I told her. I reached down and grasped her beneath her arms, pulling her to her feet in the tub. Her body glistened as the water ran down in rivulets, flowing between her full breasts back into the tub. When the air touched her breasts her nipples sprang to life as if by some silent command, and goose bumps appeared on her flesh.

"Clint, I'm cold," she complained.

"Out of the tub," I instructed. "I'll warm you."

She stepped from the tub and I reached for a towel and began to dry her, slowly, tantalizingly. First her back and her shoulders, to cut down on the chill; then I ran the towel lovingly over her breasts, cupping them through the fabric, tweaking the nipples. She squirmed against me, getting me wet, whispering, "Your clothes."

"Not yet," I said. "I'm not finished."

I went down to my knees and dried her belly and her navel, and then I ran the towel through her pubic hair. Using two fingers, I found her stiff little love button and began to massage it, still using the towel.

"Oh," she gasped, widening her eyes. "My legs are getting weak."

"So lie down," I said. When she moved for the bed I held her fast and said, "Not there. On the floor."

"Clint—" she said, but I increased the pressure of my fingers and she gasped again and sank to the floor.

With my right hand between her legs, rubbing against her, I used my other hand and the rest of the towel to dry her thighs and legs. Once that was done, I reached up and began to massage her breasts as well, concentrating on her nipples, while I continued my ministrations below her waist.

Her body was straining against my hands and she was whimpering and grabbing for me through my clothing.

"Please," she whispered. "Please, let me . . . oh, oh, ohhh!"

Due to the constant pressure of my fingers, her body shuddered with orgasm, and she closed her eyes and gave herself up to it, totally. For a moment

I thought she had lost consciousness, but then her eyes fluttered open and she began to catch her breath.

"My God," she said as I helped her to her feet. "I've never—nobody's ever done that—and with a towel!"

I turned her around to dry her back from the floor, then dropped the towel, reached around and cupped her breasts in my hands as I kissed her neck. I took the nipples firmly between my thumb and forefingers and twirled them, causing her to catch her breath again. She pushed back against me, rubbing her buttocks against the bulge in my pants, and she said, "Will you please take your clothes off!"

"Sure," I said. "Why didn't you ask before?"

I released her and removed my clothing, and then as I reached for her again she moved towards the bed, with me trailing behind her.

"Let's do it right, this time," she said.

"Let's do it different," I replied. She frowned at me, lying down on her back, but I took her hips in my hands and turned her over onto her belly.

"What are you—"

I positioned myself over her and ran my erection over the cheeks of her buttocks and then along the crack between them. I dipped between her thighs, then took her hips in my hands and raised her up. I found her moist portal from behind and rammed myself home, and she stiffened, gripped the sides of the bed and screamed into her pillow.

"My God!" she rasped as I began to move in and out of her. The angle of penetration was totally different from this position, and apparently it was one she had never experienced before.

As I drove into her she began to respond by

driving herself back against me, and soon the room was filled with the sound of flesh slapping against flesh, and her deep moans of pleasure.

"Do you want to turn over?" I asked her at one point.

"No, no," she cried out. "Do it to me this way! Come in me this way! I want to feel it."

She wriggled against me, and I continued to drive myself into her, faster and faster. She climaxed first, with a great, shuddering ripple of her muscles, and then I let myself go, firing my seed into her with such force it was almost painful.

"Oh, yes," she cried out. "Yes, yes, don't stop!"

I wished I could oblige her, but I had to empty out sometime, and eventually the end came.

I stayed inside her and began to knead her shoulder muscles, her back and then her buttocks, which brought a great moan from her again.

"Oh God, where did you learn all of this?" she asked me. "I've never met a man who tried so hard to give pleasure to a woman."

"If I feel good, I want you to feel good, too," I answered. "It's that simple." I continued to massage her buttocks and lower back, simply because I liked the way her behind felt in my hands.

"Mmm," she said, spreading her arms wide and grinding herself into the sheets. "I must say you certainly know how to take someone's mind off of . . . things."

"We're not supposed to be thinking about . . . things," I said, mimicking her tone.

"I should be giving you some pleasure, too, though," she complained. "I feel like all I'm doing is taking."

"Believe me," I said, "I enjoyed this just as much as you did."

She reached down between her legs with her right hand and caught me at the base of my penis, which was still inside of her. She wrapped a couple of fingers around me and began working my tool in and out of herself again, saying, "You are a lovely, lovely man, Clint Adams. Oh, it's growing again, isn't it?"

"It sure is," I agreed, feeling myself beginning to swell inside of her again. I ran my hands up her back, beneath her arms, down over her breasts and settled on her hips, which I gripped tightly so that I could drive myself into her again.

After a few moments of that she gasped, "Let me turn over."

I withdrew only long enough for her to do so and then quickly spread her legs and pushed myself home again. She gripped my head in her hand and covered my mouth with her full, succulent lips. I sucked on her tongue as she sucked me deeper into her and literally pulled my orgasm from me.

"Oh God," she moaned again as we rested in each other's arms. "Why couldn't we be somewhere else?"

"Do you want to leave?" I asked.

She smiled slyly and said, "I didn't say that. After all, I am a gambler, and there's a big score to be had . . . but maybe after?"

"Sure," I agreed, letting one of her nipples tickle the palm of my hand. "After."

"Clint?"

"Hmm?"

"What's going on?"

"What do you mean?"

"You know what I mean," she said. "What happened to Von Baulmer?"

"Diana—"

"Now don't put me off," she said, sternly. "I'm not going to go and tell anyone if you don't want me to, but I want to know. God, all I want to know is what you know. Is that so unfair?"

"I suppose not," I said.

"Well?"

If we had been anywhere else, I might have been able to keep putting her off, but lying there in bed with her I somehow felt compelled to tell her the truth.

"All right," I said. "He was . . . strangled."

"But who?" she said. "Why?"

"I don't know who *or* why," I said.

"Somebody—" she started, then stopped and shivered. I gathered her into my arms and she said, "Was it somebody . . . in the house?"

"Who knows?"

"Well, who's trying to find out?" she demanded.

"The sheriff is conducting an investigation."

."Him?" she said, laughing. "He couldn't—wait a minute. You used to be a lawman. *You* could find out."

I laughed softly and said, "I'm flattered at your confidence in me, but I'm in the same fix as the sheriff. I was a lawman, but not a detective."

"But you're smart," she said. "Smarter than he is, surely."

"I'm not at all sure whether that's a compliment or not," I replied.

She slapped my wrist and said, "Be serious."

"I am."

"No, you could do it. I know you could."

"It's the sheriff's job," I said.

"Pooh," she said, and then she stopped, as if something had just occurred to her. "Wait a second."

"What?"

"Breakfast."

"It's not time yet."

"No, I mean this morning—yesterday morning. You were questioning Joseph."

"Curiosity."

She looked at me slyly now, as if we shared a secret and said, "Sure, curiosity. I feel better, Clint, knowing that you're here and you're investigating—"

"Diana, I might ask a few questions, and keep my ears open, but that doesn't constitute an investigation."

"Have it your way," she said, snuggling against me. "But I hope you don't mind if I feel a little more comfortable with you being here."

"I don't mind at all," I said, really rather comfortable myself.

"And let's not worry about what anyone will think," she suggested. "Stay until morning?"

"What about your reputation?" I teased.

"I'd much rather feel safe," she said. "Let's take a chance, shall we?"

"I'm at your service."

She closed her eyes and in a few moments her breathing was even and deep, and she was asleep.

I thought back to what I said about asking questions and keeping my ears open, and realized that it sounded like a pretty accurate definition of an investigation, to me.

FOURTEEN

We went down for breakfast together, and aside from a few raised eyebrows, nobody seemed outraged.

"You see?" she whispered.

"But who knows what they're thinking?" I replied.

"Who cares?"

We breakfasted with half the players while the other half were still in their rooms.

"You look well rested, Mr. Adams," Barnaby said from across the table. "As do you, Miss Caine."

"I slept very comfortably, thank you," she replied.

"I don't think I've ever seen you look lovelier," he said, as if he'd known her all her life. "There is a glow on your cheeks."

"Eat your breakfast, Mr. Barnaby," she told him. "It's getting cold."

He smiled and proceeded to do just that.

"He's a smart man," she said to me as she filled her own plate.

"And a damned good card player."

"Is he really? I've never played with him, but he has a reputation for being sharp."

"He is," I assured her.

"Well, that's all right, then," she said, pouring herself a cup of coffee.

"What's all right?"

She smiled and said, "I thought taking this game was going to be too easy, but now that I know that Barnaby is all they say he is, it will be more interesting."

"You're pretty confident, aren't you?"

"I'm the Wild Bill Hickok of poker," she said, proudly.

I grinned and said, "I'm sure Bill will be very interested in that comparison."

Her eyes widened and she said, "You know him?"

"We've been down the road a couple of times together," I said. Before she could ask another question I said, "What about the people at your table?"

"No problem," she assured me, digging into her breakfast.

"Tyson?"

"He's not a bad player, actually—" She suddenly looked past me and stopped short.

"What?" I said, looking behind me. It wasn't until that very moment that I realized that my back had been to the door, which sent chills down my spine.

The look on Tyson's face as he stood in the doorway of the dining room told me that he was feeling some chills too.

"Tyson?"

"Uh, Mr. Adams, could I see you for a moment?" he said, hesitantly.

"Of course," I said, rising.

"Is there something that the rest of us should know?" Barnaby asked very loudly. The others at the table—Diana, Monte Blake, Pop Walen—all looked at Tyson expectantly.

"Uh—" was all he could say, and then his eyes looked at me, pleading for help.

"Why don't you let me talk to Mr. Tyson," I said to Barnaby. "If there's something you should know, I'll tell you."

Barnaby traded stares with me for a few moments, then said, "Well, sure."

I looked at Diana, then left the table and went into the foyer with Tyson.

"What's wrong?"

"A-another one," he stammered.

"What?"

"There's been another . . . k-killing."

"Who?"

"The Frenchman, Pleshette."

"Show me his room," I said.

I followed him upstairs and down the hall, past my room to one two doors down from mine, next to Blake's room. I opened the door and stepped in, and he was lying on his left side in the bed.

"Stay outside," I instructed, and he did so, gratefully.

I approached the bed and leaned over him without touching him. There were no marks that I could see, but when I took a closer look at his neck, I saw the swelling and the cord.

He'd been killed in exactly the same way as Klaus Von Baulmer.

I turned and went back to the door, closing it with myself and Tyson on the outside.

"Send for the sheriff."

"Is he—"

"He's dead," I confirmed. "Killed the same way as Von Baulmer."

"My God," he said. "Why?"

"I don't know," I replied. "But we may have somebody on our hands who doesn't like foreigners."

FIFTEEN

"Two in two nights?" Fulton said as he arrived. "I don't need this, Adams."

"None of us do," I said. "Come on. I'll show you where he is."

There was another man with him, a short, grizzled old coot carrying a doctor's bag.

"This is Doc Fletcher. He agreed to come out with me and look at the body."

"Did he look at Von Baulmer, as well?"

"I did," the doctor spoke up, "and I don't like being talked about like I'm not here, young fella."

"Sorry, Doc," I said, taking an instant liking to him. "Come on, I'll show you both where he is."

As we started up the stairs I stopped and looked at Tyson, who seemed unsure about whether or not to accompany us.

"Mr. Tyson, I think your other guests deserve to know what's going on."

"I—uh, very well. I will inform them."

"Good," I said. He still seemed hesitant, so I said, "I don't think we'll need you upstairs."

"Oh, all right," he said, but he stood there and watched us walk up the stairs."

"What's the matter?" Fulton asked me.

"Why do you ask?"

"You look like you got something on your mind."

"Yeah? Well how does two dead bodies do for a start?" I asked.

He accepted that and we continued on to Pleshette's room. What had actually been on my mind, though, was Tyson's sudden transformation—again. The man was exhibiting two different personalities, and I couldn't help but wonder which was the real Tyson.

"This door."

"Where's your room?" Fulton asked as I pushed the door open.

"My room?" I asked, surprised at the question. "We just passed it."

"You didn't hear anything last night?"

"Uh—well, I wasn't in my room last night. But let's talk about that later, all right?"

He gave me a suspicious look, but agreed, and we entered the room.

"There he is, Doc," I said.

"I can see," he replied testily.

Fulton leaned over to me while the doctor examined the body, and said, "He's mad because I took him out of the saloon to bring him here."

I nodded and kept my eyes on the doc, who seemed to know what he was doing. He examined the body just as it was, then rolled it over onto its back.

"Same as the other one," he said, still bent over the bed. He prodded and poked and then stood up straight and folded his arms across his chest.

"You didn't have to drag me all the way out here to tell you this man is dead," he complained.

"Doc," Fulton said, in an exasperated tone. I suspected he had been listening to the doc's belly-aching all the way out from town.

"All right, all right," Fletcher said. "He's dead, strangled with a piece of cord, just like the other one."

"Can you tell us anything else?" I asked.

He looked at me, and I could see him wondering why he should tell me anything.

"It's all right, Doc," Fulton said. "This here's Clint Adams. He's helping me out."

"Adams?" the doctor said, and recognition was written all over his face. "Ain't you the feller they call the Gunsmith?"

"That's right."

"Well, what are you doing here? I thought these people were gamblers, not gunmen."

"Doc," Fulton said, warningly.

"I know, mind my own business," the old man said. "I could use a drink."

"When we get back to town. Can you tell us something else?" the sheriff asked.

"Only that whoever strangled these two fellers sure is strong. He damn near lopped their heads off. If he'd used a bailing wire or somethin' like that, he'd'a done just that."

"Then you don't think it could have been a woman?" I asked.

"Not unless she was seven and a half feet tall," he answered.

Fulton and I looked at each other when he said

that, because we both knew someone who was seven and a half feet tall, and it wasn't a woman.

"Sinclair," I said, and he nodded.

"That big fella, right? That's his name?"

"Yeah, but let's not jump to any conclusions here," I suggested.

"Who else could it be?" he asked. "That crazy little man—what's his name?"

"Rollo," I answered. "And there's a lot more people in this house that it could be, Sheriff."

He made a face and said, "Yeah."

"Or it could even be someone from outside the house," I added.

"But why?"

"I don't know. Maybe it's someone who wasn't invited to the game and wants to get back at Tyson."

"If that's it, then why don't he just kill Tyson?"

"I don't know," I said again. "I'm just throwing out possibilities. It could also be someone who doesn't like foreigners."

"Foreigners?"

"Von Baulmer was German, and now Pleshette, the Frenchman."

"This fella was French, huh?"

"That's right."

"Are there any other foreigners in the house?"

"Not among the players," I said. "I don't know where Tyson's people are from, but none of the other players are foreigners."

"Then maybe there won't be any more killings," he said hopefully.

"I hope not," the doc spoke up. "I don't want to be drug out here everytime somebody gets killed. Can we get back to town now? I need that drink."

"All right," Fulton said. "I brung the undertaker's wagon with me this time, so I won't need any of Mr. Tyson's people to come back to town with me—especially that big one."

"Fine," I said. "Let's go downstairs and get to it."

On the way down Fulton said, "Have you found out anything yet?"

"Not really, but I think we found out something now, thanks to the doc, here."

"What's that?"

"We've eliminated at least one suspect."

"The woman? I don't agree. She could just be a pretty strong gal," he suggested.

"Well, then, there's another way we've eliminated her."

"How's that?"

"I told you last night I wasn't in my room," I said. "That's because I was in hers."

"All night?"

"All night."

"I'll have to ask her about that, you know," he said.

"That's all right. Neither one of us will be embarrassed by it."

"I'll talk to her before I leave," he said. As we reached the stairway and started down he said, "If that's true, though, then we also eliminated another suspect, didn't we?"

"Who's that?"

"You," he said. "Ain't that convenient?"

"Yeah," I said. "I guess it is."

SIXTEEN

Fulton was true to his word, and he questioned Diana again before he left with the doctor, who bellyached some more about having to drive the wagon.

"It's thirsty work," I reminded him outside the house. "Just think of the drink that's waiting for you at the other end."

He thought about it and then said, "You're pretty smart, for a young fella."

I had my doubts about that, but agreed to humor him.

Fulton finally came out of the house and approached me.

"The lady backs up your story, Adams," he said.

"Was there ever any doubt in your mind?"

"Just because I asked you to help don't mean that you can't be the killer, you know," he said.

"And what do you think now?"

"You and the girl clear each other—unless you're in it together," he added, frowning.

"You're confusing yourself, Sheriff," I warned him.

"And I don't need no help, believe me," he said. "You find out anything, you let me know."

"I might be coming into town a little later," I said as he mounted up.

"Oh? What for?"

"I sent some telegrams day before yesterday, and I should have gotten some answers by now. I told the clerk I'd be out here, but..." I finished by shrugging.

"If you talked to Willy Johnson," he said, going on to describe the man I'd spoken to perfectly, "then you might have a wait. He's a lazy cuss."

"Thanks. Now I'm sure I'll be going into town later."

"I'll see you there," he said. "Let's go, Doc."

"About time," the thirsty doctor said, and they started off.

While I was standing there staring after them Diana came out and joined me.

"Not another one," she said.

"I'm afraid so."

"Killed the same way?"

"Yes. I've just been thinking," I went on, "Pleshette's room was right next to mine. Maybe if I'd been there—"

"You might have heard something?"

"Maybe."

"And maybe you would have been the one to get killed," she said. "You were with me, Clint, and I'm not going to let you blame either one of us for Pleshette's death."

"No, I guess you're right."

"Besides," she added, "I don't want any kind of a shadow passed over what we had last night."

"All right," I said, putting my hand on her shoulder. "I don't want that, either. Where is our host?"

"He's in the dining room with the others, telling them what happened," she said.

"Is Talon there?"

"Talon?" She thought a moment. "I don't remember seeing him. Why?"

"I know him from somewhere, and I still can't put my finger on it. I'd better head into town," I said, suddenly deciding to go a lot sooner than I had planned.

"What for?"

"I sent some telegrams the other day, and I want to see if I got any answers. If I did, it may clear some things up."

"I'm coming with you," she said firmly.

"I don't think—"

"Don't think for one minute that I'm going to stay here without you," she broke in.

Since Diana was the one person I was sure wasn't the killer, maybe it was safer for her to be with me as much as possible. "All right, let's mount up and ride for town."

She was already wearing her riding clothes, obviously having intended to take a ride anyway.

"Shouldn't we tell Tyson?"

"I don't think we'll tell anyone, just now," I said. "Since we were together last night, Diana, we are the only ones we can trust. For a while I think we'll just keep our actions to ourselves."

SEVENTEEN

The telegram I was really hoping would come through for me was the one I had sent to Lieutenant Bill Fredericks, in Washington. Bill was an old friend of mine, and I was hoping he could snoop around in some federal files and see if he came up with anything on Deke Talon.

"Are we in the clear, as far as Fulton is concerned?" Diana asked, breaking into my thoughts. I slowed Duke a bit to keep pace with her bay so we could talk.

"Unless he believes that we're in on it together."

"He can't think that."

"I don't think he does, either," I agreed.

"Do you think anyone will pull out?"

"You said it yourself last night," I reminded her. "There's a big score to be had here."

"Yeah, but two of the players—and their money—are gone."

"There's still a lot of money left in the game, Diana."

"Don't I know it."

"Still, I think if one or two of the players do pull out, it might make the rest go too. If the pot gets cut in half, the size of the score may not be worth the risk."

"Would Fulton let them leave, though?"

I shrugged. "Could he stop them all if they wanted to go? One way or another somebody would get away."

"Maybe the murderer will be the one to try the hardest," she suggested.

"He might be the one to try the least."

"What do you mean?"

"He may not be finished yet," I said.

She fell silent after that remark, probably doing just what I said—weighing the size of the pot against the risk.

As we arrived in town I said, "You might want to do some shopping while we're here."

"I think I'll stay with you."

"I'm going to check on those telegrams and then go to the saloon for a drink."

"I've been in a saloon before," she said, giving me an amused look.

"I'm sure you have."

We rode up to the telegraph office and dismounted. She tied off her bay and I simply draped Duke's rein over the hitching rail.

"He'll walk away," she warned.

"He wouldn't dare," I told her, and she raised her eyebrows and shrugged her shoulders.

Inside Willy Johnson was standing behind the desk.

"Hi, remember me?" I asked.

He looked at me without expression for a moment, and then recognition dawned on him, and so did something else—something that looked suspiciously like fear.

"Oh, y-yes," he stammered. "H-hello."

"Did I get any answers on those telegrams I sent?"

"Telegrams," he repeated.

"Yes, those telegrams I sent day before yesterday. I told you where I would be if I got any answers. Remember?"

"Oh, sure, sure, I remember," he said quickly. "I remember."

We stood there staring at each other as I waited for answer. When I realized that we were both waiting for the other to speak I said, "Well?"

He jumped nervously and started to stammer again.

"I—I—uh, no answer—"

I grabbed the front of his shirt and hauled him halfway across the counter.

"Did you even send those telegrams?"

"I—I—"

I shook him back and forth and up and down a bit, but all I brought out of him were a few more "I—I's" until he sounded as if he were saying "Ay-yi-yi."

"I guess that answers my question," I said, dropping him onto the floor.

"He'd kill me," the clerk said, finally giving me something.

"Who would kill you?" I asked.

"I can't—I can't—" he said, stammering again.

"He's obviously afraid of someone," Diana said from behind me. "Probably even more than he's afraid of you."

At that moment I wished I were the type of man who used his gun to make threats. I could have drawn it out and put it in his mouth and seen just how much more afraid he was of that other person than he was of me and my gun.

Unfortunately, I had made a lifelong practice of never drawing my gun unless I intended to use it, and I very rarely broke that practice.

"All right," I told the shaking clerk. "All right." I turned to Diana and said, "Come on."

"What now?" she asked. "Why don't you make him send the messages now?"

"Do you know how to work a telegraph key?" I asked her.

"No."

"Neither do I. He could rattle that key off and I'd never know if he was sending or not. Come on, let's get a drink."

We went to the saloon which, although crowded and lively, quieted down a bit when Diana made her entrance with me. They looked her over for a while, then me, and then went back to what they were doing.

I ordered a couple of beers and we took them to a corner table, which was conveniently empty.

"Do you suppose Talon is the one who got to the clerk?" Diana asked.

"That'd be my bet," I said. "Although it's just as likely that Tyson himself, or one of his minions, got to him. After all, it's his town."

Just then I noticed a couple of hardcases seated a couple of tables over, giving Diana the eye. They were checking me out and trying to decide if it was worth the trouble to come over.

I hoped, for their sakes, that they would decide against it.

Hoped against hope, I should have said. No sooner had I put my beer mug down than both of them stood up and started to mosey over.

"Just sit tight," I said to Diana. "And don't say anything."

"What—" she started, but caught herself when the two men reached the table. She looked up at their grinning faces, then looked straight at me, ignoring them.

"Hi, baby," one of them—the taller by about five inches—said.

"Mmm, you sure are purty," the other one, who was about five-nine, said.

"Fellas," I said quietly, "I'd advise you to go back to your table."

"Hey, mister," the taller one said, "we just wanna talk to the little lady. Why don't you go over and save our table for us, huh? When we're done with her, we'll bring her back."

"Yeah," the second man agreed, still grinning at Diana.

"I don't think you two jaspers understood what I meant," I said, more forcefully. "The lady is with me. Go back to your table."

Now the two of them exchanged glances, and then both looked at me.

"You talk mighty big, mister," the taller one said. "Can you back it up?"

"I would prefer not to."

"He would prefer not to," he said to his partner. "He talks real purty, don't he."

"Not as purty as this little gal looks, though,"

the other man answered. He reached out to touch
Diana's hair, and she moved very fast. Her right
hand came across and landed on his left cheek with
a loud, resounding slap. There was a lot of force
behind the blow, because he staggered back a few
steps before catching his balance.

"Why you—" he said, his face red all over, but
redder where she had hit him.

I threw the contents of my beer mug into his
face, and as the other man went for his gun, I swung
the empty mug backhanded and caught him on the
top of his head. The only thing that saved him was
the fact that as he went for his gun he was moving,
and the mug glanced off the top of his head knocking
his hat off and driving him back a couple of feet.

I was on my feet now and as the tall man spread
his legs and set himself, the other man wiped the
beer from his eyes.

It was quiet now, as we faced each other, and
our side of the room had been cleared out. The two
were flanking me, but I wasn't worried about that.
I was worried that if either of them got off a shot
as I killed them, it might hit Diana.

"Diana," I said, watching both of them, "I want
you go get under the table." When she hesitated, I
snapped: "Now!" and she slid her chair back and
got underneath the table.

"It's your move boys, but I've got to tell you,
I'll kill you both before you can reach your guns."

They looked at each other as I spoke. The shorter
man had a beard, and beer was dripping from it to
the floor. The taller man had a receding hairline,
and there was a red mark where I had struck him
with the beer mug.

"Now, if one of you wants out, but the other goes for his gun, you both die, so you better get your signals straight right now. If you want to do this, the first move is yours."

All I had to do now was wait for them to make up their minds. Their eyes kept jumping back and forth between me and each other and I stood as relaxed as I could. We had passed the point where I was worried about their abilities with a gun. If either one of them had any confidence at all, it all would have been over by now. Their hesitation told me that I could take them both, so now it was just a matter of whether or not I would have to.

That was up to them—one of them.

The taller man was apparently the leader, because he made the decision. He shifted his feet, and then took a backward step, and I knew that was it. He followed that step with another, and then another, and his bearded friend started to move sideways, around the table. The tall man was only a few steps from the door when he turned and ran out. When his friend saw that, his mouth dropped open and he raised his hands in the air and took off.

"You can come out now," I told Diana.

She peeked up over the edge first, then stood up.

Activity started up in the saloon again, and people began to move back to their tables.

"Sit down," I told her, and she did so. I waved to the bartender and signaled for two more beers, and then sat back down myself.

"That was very impressive," she said. "Would you have been able to kill them both?"

"Definitely."

"You're very confident."

"As confident as you are in your ability to play cards."

The bartender brought the two beers and backed away from the table, staring at me. There were a few other people in the room staring at me, but I ignored them.

Diana was staring at me, too, thoughtfully.

"No," she said finally.

"No what?" I asked.

Shaking her head, she said, "I don't think I'm quite that confident. I don't think anyone can be."

I shrugged, and sipped my fresh beer.

EIGHTEEN

I expected the attention being paid me in the saloon to die down, but when it didn't I said to Diana, "It's time to go."

"You're the boss."

When we left, the stares of the men were split about evenly between Diana and me. We had both made quite an impression.

"Let's go and talk to Fulton," I suggested.

"Lead on."

When we reached the sheriff's office we found Fulton seated behind his desk, looking harried.

When he looked up and saw me he said, "You're early."

"I couldn't wait," I said.

"Did you get your answer?"

"No," I said, approaching his desk. "Someone kept my telegrams from being sent."

"Who?"

"Damned if I know, but it was someone who scared the hell out of the operator."

Fulton frowned and rubbed his hand over the stubble that covered his jaw.

"Would the answer to this message help us find out who killed them two men?"

"Not necessarily," I told him. "Did the doctor take a close look at the body?"

"He's taking a good, close look at a bottle right now, over in one of the saloons, but there ain't nothing else he can tell us," Fulton said. "From what he did say, I'm ready to go out and arrest that big fella—what's his name?"

"Sinclair?" Diana asked.

"That's the one."

"Not yet, Sheriff."

"Why not."

"I just don't think you've got enough to make it stick with a court of law."

"Well, I'll tell you one thing," he said, pointing his index finger at me. "If one more man or— pardon me, ma'am—lady gets killed, I'm gonna haul that big fella in so fast it'll make his head spin."

"Just make sure you've got big enough irons to hold him," I advised.

"I wouldn't mind if he resisted," he said, drawing his gun. "Even a little."

I don't like guns in the hands of fools, and anyone who would draw a gun when they don't need to is a fool.

"Put that thing away, Sheriff," I said, in a cold voice. Hell, my tone must have been like ice because he got this flat expression on his face and holstered his gun pretty damn quick.

"I'm sorry," I said, "but I don't think a gun

should be drawn unless a man is prepared to use it."

"That's all right," he said, staring at me. "Makes sense to me."

"We'll be going back to the house now, Sheriff," I told him. "If I come up with anything, I'll let you know."

"Sure."

"Maybe I'll even have a talk with Sinclair."

"Fine."

We said our good-byes, and I took Diana's arm and led her out onto the boardwalk.

"Jesus," she said. "You scared the pants off him."

"I guess."

"You scared me pretty good, too," she added. "The coldness in your voice."

"Yeah," I said, taking her arm again. "Come on, let's go back to the house."

After that, I had a feeling that the sheriff and I wouldn't work so well together anymore.

Diana and I rode most of the way back in a kind of strained silence, which I broke before we reached the house.

"Don't tell me I've alienated you, too?"

"No," she said. "But I've seen a couple of sides of you today that will take some getting used to."

"Will that be a problem?"

She looked up at the sky, then at me and said, "I don't think so—as long as I never pull a gun unless I intend to use it."

NINETEEN

When we got back to the house and I'd unsaddled both horses and tended to them, I said, "Why don't you go up to your room and lock the door?"

"Oh, no," she said, shaking her head emphatically. "I go where you go, Mr. Gunsmith."

I winced at the name, but I had to admit it was probably part of the reason she felt so safe with me.

"I'm still going to have to talk with Sinclair," I warned her.

"That's all right," she said. "We can balance that off."

"How?"

She smiled and said, "We'll have to talk with Rollo right after."

I laughed and said, "Let's go."

As we turned to walk from the stable, a large figure loomed in the doorway. With the sun at his back, we couldn't make out his face, but that wasn't necessary. We only knew one man who stood that big and tall.

"Sinclair," I said.

"Mr. Tyson wants to talk to you," he thundered.

"Well, I think maybe you and I will have a talk first. What do you say?"

"Mr. Tyson wants to talk to you," he said again.

"Uh-huh," I said, looking over at Diana. She shrugged and raised her eyebrows at me.

"I think maybe you and I could have that talk after I see Mr. Tyson," I said to him. "What do you say to that?"

"Mr. Tyson—"

"Lead the way, Sinclair," I said, cutting him off before he could repeat himself again. "Let's go and talk to Mr. Tyson."

He turned and started back to the house, and as we followed Diana whispered to me, "You handled that very well."

"Now all I need is for Rollo to kick me in the knee and tell me to mind my own business," I replied.

She laughed, stifling it with her hands, and we continued to follow the big man to the house.

He took us in through a back door and down a hall and brought us to what appeared to be Tyson's den. I surmised that had we entered the house from the front door, we would have gone to the right, opposite the dining room.

"Ah, Mr. Adams, Miss Caine, you're back. I was beginning to worry about you," Tyson said, smiling broadly. "That'll be all, Sinclair."

Tyson had undergone another miraculous transformation, and was once again the self-assured builder of Two Queens, Nevada.

"I'd like to talk to him a little later, if you don't

mind," I said to Tyson before the big man could leave.

Tyson looked at me, then said to Sinclair, "When Mr. Adams wants to talk, you'll oblige him Sinclair. Is that clear?"

I didn't hear the big man speak, nor did I see him move a muscle, but somehow he managed to answer his employer, who seemed satisfied and said, "Good. You can go."

Turning to us, he said, "As I stated, I was beginning to worry about the two of you. Where did you get off to?"

"We went for a ride, Mr. Tyson," I said. "I was unaware that we had to account to you for our every move."

"Not at all, not at all," he said, expansively. "But in light of recent, er, occurrences, I would think it wise for all of us to stay near the house."

"You're the host," I said. "Whatever you think is best."

"Well, to tell you the truth, Mr. Adams," he said, not looking so sure of himself now, "I was hoping you would be able to tell me what was best."

"In what way?"

"The poker game," he answered. "Shall I call it off?"

"Are you asking me as a player, or as an impartial observer?" I asked.

"As an ex-lawman who has dealt with violent situations before," he said.

"I see," I said. I looked at Diana, and then back to Tyson. "Have you asked the players if they want to continue?"

"I have, and they all do," he said. "But I would feel responsible if anyone else were to..."

"You would also feel responsible if you allowed a killer to get away, wouldn't you?"

"What do you mean?"

"If you call off the game, the people in this house would scatter. Oh, Sheriff Fulton would do his best to keep them around, but he wouldn't be able to watch them all. Even if one managed to slip out of town—"

"—that one might be the killer," he finished for me. "I see your point. Yes, of course I'll allow the game to continue."

"Good."

I didn't bother to mention that even if all of the players did leave the house, the killer might still be there. I didn't mention that because, for all I knew, I could have been talking to the killer right there and then.

Still, Sinclair was a riper suspect.

"I'd like to talk to Sinclair now, if I could," I said.

"Why?"

"I'm talking to everyone in the house, Mr. Tyson," I explained. "I've already spoken to Joseph, and to you. Now I'd like to talk to Sinclair, and then I'll talk to Rollo. Who does the cooking, by the way?"

"Mrs. Bell," he said. "She's quite elderly, however."

"That would tend to rule her out, then," I said. "Where would I find Sinclair now?"

"In the barn, I'd imagine," he said. "He likes horses very much."

"My horse—" I started to say.

"He has specific instructions not to touch your animal, Mr. Adams—although I'd dare say that your horse would be the only one that could comfortably carry a man of his size."

"I'd say so, too," I agreed, which made me even more anxious to find him at that moment.

"Miss Caine, would you like to stay with me and have a glass of brandy?" Tyson invited Diana.

"I'd love to, Mr. Tyson, but I have to go with Mr. Adams," she explained. "I'm afraid he'd be lost without me," she confided.

"I see," he said, in confusion.

"See you tonight, Mr. Tyson," I said. "At the tables."

"Yes, indeed," he replied. "Tonight."

"Come on," I said to Diana, taking her arm.

Outside the room she said, "Why the big hurry? He said Sinclair is in the stable."

"I know," I said. "And so is Duke."

"So?"

"So we'd better get there first before one of them meets his match."

TWENTY

We hurried to the stable, but uppermost in my mind now was the welfare of Duke. Talking to Sinclair was secondary for the moment.

"You don't think he'd actually try to ride Duke, do you?" Diana asked.

"I hope not," I answered. "But if he does one of them is liable to end up with a broken back."

When we got to the stable it wasn't very hard to find Sinclair. He towered above the stalls and some of the horses.

"Sinclair," I called.

He looked my way, staring for a few moments, then backed out of the stall he was in—which wasn't Duke's, I was gratified to see—and walked toward us.

"I have some questions I'd like to ask you, Sinclair."

He set his feet and put his massive hands on his hips. It was easy to imagine those hands squeezing the life out of a man's body.

"Mr. Tyson says I'm supposed to answer," he

said in his rumbling bass. "So ask."

"Where do you sleep?"

"Here."

"Here, in the stable?"

"I like horses," he said. "I like to be close to them. I like them better than people."

"Well, I can't say I blame you for that," I said. "So, if you sleep out here, I gather you didn't hear anything the last two nights, when those men were killed."

"I heard nothing."

"Did you see anything?"

"Nothing."

"Did you go near the house at any time during the last two nights?"

He stared at me for so long without answering that I thought for a moment he hadn't heard me, but then he said, "I know what you think."

"What do I think?"

"You think that because Sinclair is so big," he said, showing me his massive hands, "that he killed those two men."

"That's not what I think at all, Sinclair," I assured him. I realized that if he got mad enough to rush us, the only hope I would have of stopping him was to shoot him, and I didn't want to do that.

"Just settle down for a minute," I said, trying to make sure he didn't get riled. "I'm asking everyone questions, not just you. I questioned Joseph and even Mr. Tyson, and after I'm finished here I'm going to question Rollo."

"Rollo," he said, showing distaste. It was the first real expression I'd seen on his face since meeting him. "He is a cruel little man. Maybe he killed

those two men. He has big, strong hands for someone so small. You noticed?"

Actually, I had noticed the size of Rollo's hands,
in proportion to the rest of him, but the thought had
never occurred to me that he might be the killer.

"Yes," I answered him. "I had noticed."

"And he sleeps in the house," he added.

It occurred to me also that Sinclair seemed to
dislike Rollo a little more than just "people," and
that he could simply be trying to make trouble for
him. Still, what he said made sense. Rollo did have
better access to the house than he did.

"All right, Sinclair," I said. "Thanks for talking
to me."

"Mr. Tyson wanted me to."

"Do you always do everything Mr. Tyson wants
you to do, Sinclair?" I asked.

"Always."

"You can go back to work, Sinclair."

He nodded and began to back away, but I called
to him again when I remembered something.

"Sinclair, about my horse—"

"Mr. Tyson says I don't touch him, then I don't
touch him," he said. "He is a beautiful animal. I
will not touch him, but I would not let anything
happen to him."

"I appreciate that, Sinclair," I said, not doubting
his sincerity at all.

"It is not for you," he said. "It is for the horse.
I will go back to work now."

"Fine. I'll tell Mr. Tyson you were very—" I
began, but I stopped when I realized that we had
ceased to exist for him.

"Let's go," I told Diana, who had been silent during the entire conversation.

"He scares me," she said, "but he seemed so different, gentler, when he was talking about horses."

"Yeah," I agreed. "A guy who likes horses can't be all bad."

"He doesn't seem to like little Rollo at all," she commented.

"Yeah, I noticed that, too, but he had a point."

"Do you really think Rollo would be strong enough to strangle two full-grown men?"

"I don't know. He does have pretty large hands, though."

"I hadn't noticed."

"Well, you can take a look right now. Let's go find him and see what he has to say."

TWENTY-ONE

Rollo was a little harder to track down than Sinclair had been. When we couldn't find him ourselves I decided to see if Joseph could help us.

"Joseph," I said, when we found him in the dining room. He looked up guiltily from what he had been doing, and I realized that we had caught him counting the silverware.

"Sir," he said. He had some forks in his hands and he hastily put them down on the table.

"Counting the silver, Joseph?" Diana asked, sounding amused. "Don't you trust Mr. Tyson's guests?"

"If one of them would kill someone," he reasoned, "certainly stealing would not be beyond them."

"I suppose that makes a lot of sense," I said.

"Yes, sir."

"All right, Joseph. Could we take you away from your counting for a moment?"

"Sir?"

"Have you seen Rollo today?"

"No, thank God," he replied.

"What?"

Joseph's icy composure disappeared, and he looked like a conspiratorial kid as he said, "May I confide in you?"

"Sure."

"I say a prayer every night that I will not see that little atrocity the next day."

"What's wrong with him?" Diana asked.

Joseph barely suppressed a shiver and said, "He's hideous!"

"Well, he is rather...unusual looking," Diana replied, looking at me and shrugging.

"I don't mean physically," Joseph said. "Although one can't deny that he is repulsive in that sense. However, I was speaking more of his soul."

"His soul?" I asked.

"It's black," he said. "That little man is the evilest person I have ever had the displeasure of meeting."

"How long has he worked here, Joseph?" I asked.

"He came here three months ago, sir."

"Was Mr. Tyson expecting him?"

"I couldn't say."

"Could you guess?"

"I would rather not," he said, and all of a sudden he was the old Joseph again. "It would not be proper."

"Where are you from, Joseph?"

"England, sir. Mr. Tyson hired me not long after I came to this country, for which I am very grateful."

"How about Sinclair?" I asked. "When did he come here?"

"Sinclair has worked for Mr. Tyson almost as long as I have."

"How long is that?"

"I have worked for Mr. Tyson for four years," he answered. "Sinclair for slightly less than that."

"What does Sinclair do?"

"He handles the horses on the ranch."

"And you handle the house?"

"Yes."

"What does Rollo do?"

He closed his eyes and this time he was able to suppress the shudder, but not without some effort.

"I do not know, sir."

"You don't know?" I asked, surprised.

"No, sir."

"Who does?"

"Only Mr. Tyson, sir."

I frowned and told Joseph, "All right, thank you, Joseph."

"Thank you, sir."

As we were leaving the room I heard the clink of the silverware as he continued his count.

"Rollo seems to be something of a mystery," Diana said as we reached the outer hall.

"Yeah," I said, and I was wondering why. "Let's go into the poker room and get a drink."

"Good idea."

When we entered the room some of the players were seated at a table, involved in a pick-up game. Monte Blake was no doubt the instigator, and he had gotten Pop Walen and Danny Rose to sit in.

"Ah, fresh blood," Blake called out as we entered. "Take a chair, you two. The more the merrier."

"No, thanks," I said, heading for the bar. Diana declined politely and followed me.

"Brandy?" I asked, positioning myself behind the bar.

"Fine."

We were far enough away from the others so that they couldn't hear us.

"I don't see Talon," she said.

"You had to remind me, didn't you?" I said, handing her a filled glass. I stared at the table of players and repeated, "You had to remind me."

TWENTY-TWO

I would be the first person to admit that I am not a gambler—at least, not in the way that the other people at those two tables were. Gambling was their business, but I was a little amazed to find that they were able to concentrate so fully on the game, in light of what had happened over the past two nights. My lack of concentration cost me half my stake that night, which bothered me, but not as much as having people die around me.

After the session—which for some reason ended a little earlier than the others—I went right to the bar for a brandy, and found myself face to face with Danny Rose. I readied myself for another round of complaining about why he lost, but I was to be surprised.

"About time those hands of mine started paying off," he said.

"I gather you won tonight?"

"And damn well about time, too," he said. "Hell, I cleaned up tonight, Adams. Made back what I lost and then some. I'm on a roll now and—"

"Excuse me," I said. "I see someone I've got to talk to."

Rose was just as bad when he won as he was when he lost.

I took my drink across the room and collared Tyson to ask him about Rollo.

"I've been trying to find him all day," I said.

"Oh, I'm sorry," he said immediately. "I should have told you earlier."

"Told me what?"

"I sent Rollo to town to do some errands for me."

"And he hasn't returned?"

"Which is no surprise," he assured me. "Very often Rollo is forced to spend the night in town to see to business matters for me."

"I see."

"I'm sorry, Mr. Adams."

"That's all right," I assured him. "No harm done."

Diana was waiting for me at the bar when I finished with Tyson, and Danny Rose was going on and on to her about how the cards finally came around and caught up with his skill.

"Diana," I said, approaching them. "Can I see you, please?"

"Of course," she said, gratefully. "Excuse me."

We left Rose standing there with no one to talk to, looking bewildered.

"Thanks," she said, holding onto my arm.

"I guess he won?"

"Big," she acknowledged. "He had an unbelievable run, Clint, and time ran out on us catching up, but we will tomorrow."

"Is he any good?"

She paused, then said, "I don't want to badmouth

anyone. I mean, his playing must have some method for him to have been invited here."

"I suppose," I said. "Although I still wonder myself why I was invited."

"You're holding your own, aren't you?"

"I was until tonight," I replied. "I simply wasn't able to concentrate on the game the way the rest of you were."

"I think you're still more lawman than you are gambler, Clint," she said, "which makes that understandable."

"But not very smart. It cost me half my stake."

"I'm sorry," she said. "Why don't we go up to my room, where we can both turn our attention to something a little more pleasant?"

"I had that in mind," I said, although the reason I wanted to go to her room with her was to make sure the two of us were safe.

I'm not saying I expected someone else to die that night; I'm just saying that I didn't want it to be either of us.

TWENTY-THREE

As soon as Diana was sound asleep, I slipped from her bed without waking her, dressed and let myself out. I hoped she wouldn't wake up until I returned. I didn't like the thought of her waking up and finding me gone, but I couldn't just lie there hoping that no one else would be killed. I had to act on the assumption that there would be another murder, and try to head it off if I could.

Now that I was in the hall, though, I wasn't sure what my best move would be. I could go back to my own room and just keep my ears open. But if I went to my room, I'd sit there worrying that I'd left Diana alone. I couldn't win.

I decided to take a walk down to the first floor and see if anyone was still awake. If no one was about and assuming then that they were all asleep, I could sit on those steps; if someone was going to get into the house, he'd have to pass me to get upstairs.

Providing the killer wasn't already in the house. . . .

I checked out the downstairs rooms—the ones

117

that weren't locked—and then sat on the steps, trying to think of something useful to do. I finally decided to go around knocking on everyone's door, to make sure they were where they should be—and alive. I might end up with a few people mad at me, but if they were angry, they were alive.

Things didn't quite work out the way I planned, though. I went back upstairs and to the right, where the men were quartered, and knocked on the first door I reached. When there was no answer, I thought that maybe I had hit pay dirt right off. I tried the door and found it unlocked. I opened it slowly and stuck my head into the dark room. There was just enough moonlight coming through a window so that I could see that no one was there. The bed had not even been slept in.

I found out the hard way that the room wasn't as empty as it looked. Sticking my head in the door was like putting it through a noose, and when something hit me on the back of the head, it was like the trapdoor dropping open beneath, and I fell through. . . .

TWENTY-FOUR

There was a lot of commotion going on some-where. People running and shouting, and that was what woke me up. I put my hand over the lump on the back of my head and staggered to my feet. Daylight filtered through the window, lighting the room, which was really empty now, except for me. I turned around and saw that the door had been closed behind me. When I opened it, the commotion was louder.

I went out into the hall and leaned my back against the wall. Down towards the end of the hall there was a crowd of people in front of one of the rooms. I saw Barnaby, Monte Blake, Pop Walen, and Tyson.

"Clint!" Diana shouted. She had come from the other direction, and when she called my name, the others looked my way also.

"There's Adams," Blake said.

Tyson saw me and came running down the hall, but Diana reached me first, grabbing onto my arm.

"Where have you been?" she demanded, sounding worried. I took my hand down from behind my head at that point, and there was blood on it.

"You're hurt!" she cried.

"Yeah," I said, blinking my eyes to try and clear away the fog.

"Mr. Adams, what happened?" Tyson demanded, reaching us.

"He's hurt," Diana told him. "He needs a doctor."

"Of course," Tyson said. "I have to send for the sheriff anyway." He looked at me and said, "There's been another murder."

"Who?"

"Daniel Rose."

"Damn!" I snapped.

"Can we take care of his head, please?" Diana asked Tyson.

"Of course," he said. "Come downstairs."

"I want to see Rose," I said.

"Clint—"

"Come on," I told Tyson. "Let's get those people away from the room until the sheriff gets here."

"Clint—" Diana said again, sounding exasperated, but I was too angry to pay attention—angry at myself for allowing Danny Rose to be killed.

"Come on," I said to the others. "Everyone away from the door."

"Where were you, Adams?" Blake asked. "Where were you when Rose was getting himself killed?"

"I was out cold, Blake," I said. "Where were you?"

I pushed past him without waiting for an answer, and saw Rose lying on the bed with a piece of cord digging into the flesh of his neck.

"Sorry, Danny," I said.

"Please, let's go downstairs," I heard Tyson telling the others. "I must send for the sheriff."

"Shut the door," I called out to him.

"You going to leave him alone in there?" Blake asked Tyson. "How do you know he didn't kill him."

"And what if he did?" Diana demanded, pushing past all of the men with a damp rag in her hand. "Is he going to kill him again if you leave him here? Go on, all of you, why don't you go downstairs." And with that she slammed the door in their faces.

"You are so stubborn, aren't you?" she asked me. She came over to me and placed the cool damp rag against the back of my head, and she did it without once looking at the body on the bed.

"I let this happen, damn it!"

"Don't talk foolish," she scolded me.

"I was up, walking around," I explained. "I was about to knock on everyone's door, to see if anyone was missing from their room. I could have kept it from happening."

"Sure, if someone hadn't tried to take your head off."

"That first room was empty," I said, looking at her. "We've got to find out whose room that is."

"Just hold on a second," she said. She removed the rag and checked the bleeding, then replaced it. "Let's see if we can stop the bleeding, and then the doctor can do the rest."

I noticed that it was taking a large effort on her part not to look at the body, so I said, "Why don't we get out of here, too?"

"Fine with me," she agreed. As we walked to

the door she asked, "Clint, was he killed the same way as the others?"

"The same way," I said.

"The poor kid."

"Yeah," I said. "If it hadn't been for my carelessness, he'd be alive now."

We stepped out into the hall and I closed the door firmly behind us.

"You don't know that you could have stopped it," she said.

"I had a damn good chance."

"You could have gotten killed yourself!" she shouted at me, thrusting the rag into my hands. "That's what I thought when I woke up and found you gone. I thought I'd never see you alive again."

I stared at her and said, "You were that concerned, huh?"

"You ass!" she said. "You horse's ass!"

"You're right about that," I agreed, dabbing at the back of my head with the rag. "I got played for a real horse's ass."

TWENTY-FIVE

When Fulton arrived he was all business. Very formal, very official.

"I'll come up with you," I said, as he came into the house with the doctor.

"Let the doctor look at you," Diana insisted.

I gave her a sharp look, but Fulton settled it by saying, "I don't need you upstairs, Adams. I know a dead body when I see one." Then he frowned at me and asked, "What do you need a doctor for?"

"Somebody hit him on the head," Diana answered before I could open my mouth.

"Doc, take a look at him, and then come upstairs," he instructed the doctor, who looked as if he'd been interrupted during another drinking binge.

"Sure," he answered, indifferently. "Come along, young fella."

Fulton went upstairs with Tyson, and I went into the dining room with Diana and the doctor, where the rest of the guests were already congregated.

"Sit right there," the doctor instructed. I sat where he indicated and he asked someone for water. Diana went into the kitchen and came out with a basin, then stood by to supervise his handiwork.

At one point he looked at her from the corner of his eyes and said, "All right with you?"

"You're doing fine," she replied.

"A hell of a lot better than Danny Rose is doing," Monte Blake muttered from the other end of the room. Diana threw him a nasty look, and I ignored him because I couldn't have moved my head to look at him, anyway.

"You going to put a bandage on it, Doc?"

"Don't need one," he said. "Somebody did a good job of stopping the bleeding before I got here."

"Thank you," Diana said.

He looked at her and said, "I figured."

He stood up straight and put his tools back in his little black bag.

"That's all I can do," he said. "I got another patient waiting upstairs."

"He ain't going anywhere," Blake put in.

"Don't be jumping around too much, son," Doc told me. "Not for a while yet." He looked pointedly at Diana and then added, "Might do you a world of good to stay in bed some."

Diana knew what the old man meant and she gave him a sweet smile and said, "I couldn't agree more."

The doctor nodded shortly and said, "I figured."

When he left I became aware of the fact that I was the center of attention in the room.

I stared right at Monte Blake and asked, "Have you got something to say, Blake?" since he was all mouth while I was being treated.

Now he backed off a bit and looked around at the others, as if waiting for one of them to speak up. When none of them volunteered, he turned and looked at me again.

"I'm just wondering where you were when Rose was getting killed, that's all," he said, finding a little extra courage somewhere. He was nervous, though. I could tell from the way he was riffling the deck he was holding in his hands.

"I told you where I was," I said. "I was on the floor of somebody's room, out cold—or do you think I hit myself behind the head after I killed him?"

"Anything's possible," he replied.

"Horseshit!" Diana looked, drawing some surprised glances, especially from Barnaby.

"Well, now," he said, deciding to put his two cents in, "I don't see how Adams could possibly have done that to himself—"

"Wait a minute," I said, interrupting him.

"I'm on your side, Adams," he said hastily.

"I appreciate that, Barnaby, but I don't really need anybody on my side," I said. "I just need the answer to one question."

"What's that?" he asked.

"Whose room was I in?" I said. "I knocked on that door and when I didn't get an answer I went on in. I had just enough time to see that the bed hadn't been slept in before someone hit me on the head. Now what I want to know is, whose room is that?"

"Well, it wasn't mine," Barnaby said, and the others exchanged glances, all shaking their heads.

"Has anybody seen Deke Talon?" I asked.

Again they exchanged glances and shook their heads.

"He's the only one left," I said. "It must be his room."

"You think Deke is liable to show up dead somewhere?" Barnaby asked.

"Actually," I said, looking at Diana, who I could see was thinking the same way I was, "that wasn't what I had in mind at all."

TWENTY-SIX

I decided that instead of sitting there trading remarks with Blake and some of the others, I'd go upstairs and see what was happening. Diana had a choice of staying with them or coming with me, which wasn't much of a choice, and we went upstairs together.

Tyson was standing outside of the room while Fulton and the doc were examining the body.

"Mr. Tyson?" I called, striding down the hall with Diana trotting along behind me.

"Mr. Adams," he replied, "are you feeling better?"

"I'm fine," I said, stopping next to him so that I could see into the room. The doc was bent over the body while Fulton was staring off into space, arms folded in front of him.

"I'm very disappointed in the way Sheriff Fulton is handling this whole affair," Tyson said to me. "I will have to take it up with the rest of the town council."

"He's not a detective, Mr. Tyson," I reminded

him. "He's just a sheriff. He's not trained to investigate—"

"That may be," he said, interrupting me, "but I am still disappointed."

"That's up to you," I said. "I have a question, though."

"What is it?"

"The room I was in when I got hit on the head," I said. "Whose room is that?"

He leaned back to peer down the hall past me and Diana, then said, "I believe that's Mr. Talon's room."

"Have you seen him today?"

He thought a moment and then said, "Now that you mention it, no, I haven't. In the face of all of the excitement, I would say that's rather odd, wouldn't you?"

"I would say so, indeed."

"Do you think he is the killer, and has fled, fearing discovery?"

"I would say he's looking pretty good right now," I said.

"What's going on?" Fulton demanded, striding out of the room into the hall with us.

"We were just noticing the absence of one of our players, Sheriff," Tyson explained.

"Who's that?"

"Deke Talon," I said. "It was his room I got knocked out in, but not before I noticed that his bed hadn't been slept in."

"Where is his room?"

"End of the hall," I said, pointing that way.

Fulton walked down the hall towards the room, and I took the opportunity to enter Rose's room.

"What do you see, Doc?"

"I see a dead man," he replied. "What do you see?"

"I see a smart-ass doctor who may have had his last drink," I replied in a flat tone.

He looked over at me to see if I was serious, then said, "Don't joke about a thing like that, son. I take my drinking very, very serious."

"That's the way I react to murder, Doc," I said.

"All right," he said, wiping his hands on a rag he'd taken from his bag. "I see a man who was killed exactly the same way as the other two, strangled by a very strong person," he said.

"Okay, thanks, Doc," I said, backing out of the room.

Fulton was back, and he asked, "Nobody has seen this guy Talon this morning?"

"That's correct."

"Well that seems to be it, then," he said, rubbing his hands together. "If we find that feller, we'll have our killer. Mr. Tyson, I'll have two of my men come up here for the body, and then we'll get on this Talon's trail."

"I appreciate you taking some kind of effective action, Sheriff," Tyson said, but his cynical tone was lost on the sheriff, who seemed to smell an imminent arrest.

"What about Sinclair, Sheriff?" I asked.

"Who?"

"The big man you were hoping would resist—"

Fulton cleared his throat to cut me off and said, "I myself saw that big feller out front when we pulled up. He ain't taking off, but this other feller Talon has. That makes him guilty in my book." He looked into the dead man's room and said, "I'll send my men up, Doc."

"Well, hurry it up, damn it. I'm thirsty."

I looked at Diana, who was suppressing a grin, and said, "I figured."

TWENTY-SEVEN

When the sheriff and the doc left with the body it got very quiet at Two Queens ranch, and with good reason. Three murders in three nights, all of the victims killed in exactly the same manner.

"Mr. Tyson," I said, as we reentered the house after seeing the body off, "I suggest we all gather in the dining room and talk about this. Let's see if someone—anyone—has some useful thoughts on the subject."

"I think that's a good idea," he agreed.

"And I mean everyone," I added. "Joseph, Sinclair, even Rollo—if he's back."

"He is back. We will all meet you there."

"Fine."

I took Diana's arm and steered her into the dining room, where Blake, Barnaby and Pop Walen were just starting to get up.

"Let's all sit back down," I said. "Tyson is rounding up everyone else and we're going to talk about this."

"He's not going to call the game off, is he?" Blake asked, looking worried.

"I think that's the least of our problems right now, Blake," I said.

"Least of yours, maybe," he said, "but it's the reason I came out here and I ain't going to leave empty-handed."

"I've got an answer to that, Blake," I told him. "But let's wait for the others."

"Who exactly are we waiting for?" he asked.

"Tyson's staff," I said.

"You mean the giant and the midget?" he said. "You think that little man might be the murderer?" he asked, laughing. "You're reaching a bit, aren't you, Adams? Besides, I heard the sheriff say he knew who the killer was."

"Talon?" I asked, and he nodded. "Just because Talon is missing doesn't mean he's the killer."

"You seemed to think so earlier," Barnaby pointed out.

"I admit the thought occurred to me," I said. "But I'm not ready to pass judgment just yet."

"So what do you propose we do?" Blake demanded.

I didn't like his tone, so I said, "I propose you shut your yap right now while we wait for the others."

Blake reacted as if I'd slapped him, but he subsided with a petulant look on his face.

After a few more tense moments, Tyson showed up with Sinclair and Rollo behind him, presenting a very odd-looking trio, indeed.

"What about Joseph?" I asked.

"Here, sir," the manservant said, coming out of the kitchen. "Do you want the cook as well, sir?"

he asked, and I wasn't sure if he was talking to me or to Tyson, but I said, "No, leave her in the kitchen."

"What's the matter, Adams?" Blake asked. "You're ready to think that a midget is the killer; what about an old lady?"

As he said that I looked at Rollo and the fury in his face was plain as day.

"Mr. Blake," he said, "I'll have to warn you about that kind of talk, or I might be tempted to come over there and show you just what a *dwarf* can do to a big windbag."

Blake was a lot braver with Rollo than he was with me—that is, until he saw the naked fury on the little man's face. It was enough to intimidate anyone, and I thought I was able to see in that moment just what Joseph had been talking about.

"Enough, Rollo," Tyson said, and *his* tone of voice surprised me. He had only said two words, but there was such force behind them that Rollo immediately relaxed and turned away from Blake.

"Mr. Tyson," I said, "this is your house, but if you don't mind, I'd like to preside at this little council of war."

"That's fine with me, Mr. Adams."

"Anybody else have any objections?" I asked, looking right at Monte Blake.

No one objected, including him.

"Fine. I'd like to know if anyone heard anything over the past three nights that might help us, no matter how insignificant it might have seemed at the time."

I could have added, "Don't everybody talk at once." In fact, I could have recited the Declaration of Independence without being interrupted.

"No one heard a thing?"

"Excuse me, Clint," Barnaby said. "But I for one sleep very soundly after eight or ten hours of intense concentration on a poker game."

Everybody seemed to jump on that as a good answer—all of the players, that is.

"Rollo," I said, picking on the little man because he had been so hard to locate, and now I had him where I wanted him.

He looked at me with raised eyebrows, and although he was only about three and a half feet tall, I got the distinct impression that he was looking down at me.

"Yes?"

"You didn't hear anything?"

"If I had, I would have spoken up when you asked, Mr. Adams," he replied. "Wouldn't I?"

"Yes, I suppose you would have."

"You know, this all seems like a waste of time to me," Blake spoke up.

"Is that so?" I said.

"Yeah. As far as I'm concerned, Talon is the killer and we can go on with our game—and on one table now."

"Is that the way you feel?" I asked the others. "Pop? Barnaby? Diana?"

I waited for an answer from each of them.

"I think maybe it's time to call it quits," Pop said finally.

"There comes a time in every game when you have to cut and run," Barnaby said.

"I don't mind saying I'm scared," Diana said.

"Mr. Tyson?" I asked.

"I will abide by the majority decision."

"You're a player, Adams," Blake said—just as I was hoping he would. "What about you?"

"I agree with you, Blake."

"You do?"

"Yes, but not for the same reasons. I think we're stronger if we stay together. Whoever the killer is, he's got something in mind for each of us, I think. If we split up, he just might track us all down and get it done anyway." I stopped and looked at all of their faces to see how they were receiving this. "I'd like to get it all resolved before I leave here, wouldn't you?"

"I'd like to leave here alive," Barnaby said.

"So would I," I agreed. "But once I leave, I want to stay alive."

"This is not fair, you know," Pop Walen said.

"What isn't?"

"You've dealt with the danger of death all your life, Adams," he said. "We're not used to that, yet you ask for us to do it anyway."

"You're wrong, Pop," I replied. "I'm not the one who put you in this position. . . . The killer is."

I looked around and decided to pick on Rollo again.

"Rollo,"

"Yes?" he replied with a tolerant look.

"Who tells you how to live your life, Rollo?"

"I do."

"Are you going to let this killer affect the way you live?"

"No."

"Why not?" I asked, looking at Pop Walen. I was trying to show Pop and the rest of them that *little* Rollo wasn't afraid of a killer, even though he was only three and a half feet tall.

All eyes were on Rollo as he answered smugly, "Because he's only killing poker players, and I don't play poker." He shook his oversized head and muttered, "Jerks," and left the room.

The silence was deafening as everyone watched Rollo walk from the room, leaving his bombshell behind him.

And quite a bombshell it was too, because it set off a chain of thought in my mind that logically brought me part of the answer.

Which I decided to keep to myself—at least until I had Diana alone and could go over it with her and see how it sounded out loud.

"All right," I said. "Let's let it lie until tonight, and we can all decide. I suggest that no one leaves the house, and if you have to, don't go alone."

"Excellent idea," Tyson said. "Thank you, Mr. Adams."

"Mr. Tyson, I suggest that those guards you have around the house during the game be put on duty permanently."

"I'll take care of it right away," he said.

"Good. I think that's it."

We looked at each other, and Sinclair was the first to break off and leave, which broke the spell. Everyone else, except for Diana and myself, began to leave.

"Pop?"

Pop Walen turned and looked at me.

"You were wrong about one thing, Pop."

"What's that?"

"We all face death everyday," I told him. "Some

of us just make a habit of getting a little closer than others."

He stood in the doorway, looking at me for a long moment, then he nodded once and left.

"Clint," Diana said, "What happened to you when Rollo answered your question and left. You looked like somebody walked over your grave."

"Not quite, Diana," I answered. "That little man just made me realize how stupid I am."

"How?" she asked, looking confused.

"What did all of the dead men have in common?"

"They all came here to play poker."

"Yeah, but something else. Think about it: Who was the big winner the first night we played?"

"I know who won at my table," she said.

"Who?"

"The German, Von Baulmer."

"Right. He was the big winner of the night. Do you know who the big winner was the next night?"

"No."

"Pleshette," I told her. "Our dead Frenchman." She started to look scared then, but I went on. "Do you know who the big winner was last night?"

"S-sure," she said. "Everyone knew. It was Danny Rose."

"And Danny Rose is dead."

TWENTY-EIGHT

It had to be somebody in the game. Who else would know who the big winner was each night? That narrowed it down to five people, after I eliminated Diana and myself.

Tyson. It was his game, which he'd been running for ten years now. If he was the killer, and word got out about what had happened—and how could it help but get out?—he would destroy his own game. What was his motive? What was worth destroying a game he'd spent ten years building up?

What would Barnaby's motive be? He was a professional. What could make him kill three people, three poker players? They were his livelihood.

Monte Blake? He wouldn't have the guts—or would he?

Pop Walen was what—sixty-seven years old or thereabouts? What could he possibly have to gain? Then again, at his age, what could he lose?

That left Deke Talon. And where was he? Who was he?

"So you're totally discounting Rollo or Sinclair?" Diana asked me.

"It has to be someone who was in the game," I reasoned.

"What about Tyson? He could have had one of them do it. They're his men, aren't they?" she asked. "Sinclair seems perfectly willing to do anything Tyson tells him to do."

"All right," I said. "Sinclair could be the tool, but Tyson would still be the killer."

"This is all very well," she said, "but how are you going to find out who the killer is, once and for all?"

"I think there's only one way," I said.

"How?"

"I've got to get everyone to play tonight, and I've got to come out as the big winner."

"You're going to ask the others to let you win?"

"I can't do that," I said. "That would be like asking the killer to let me win. No, I've got to come out the winner fair and square."

"How do you propose to do that? With my help?"

"No, I've got to do it alone," I said. "I don't want anyone to suspect, because it might put the killer off."

"I think you're crazy," she said. "You're going to make a target out of yourself, and end up getting killed for it."

"Your confidence in me is touching."

"If I hurt your feelings it's too bad, but I'd rather you get your feelings hurt than anything else."

"Look, Diana, I do enough looking over my shoulder under normal circumstances, I don't need this hanging over my head as well," I explained.

"I'm not leaving here until I find out who this killer is."

"Well, I guess if you're staying, I might as well stay too. What do you think the others will do?"

"I think they'll stay. We'll find out tonight, when we go downstairs to play. Hopefully, the others will show up as well. What I'm concerned with now is the whereabouts of Deke Talon. If he's hiding, then where?"

"Maybe he just left," she suggested. "Maybe he's the smartest one of all."

"I doubt that he's left," I said. "As for his being smart, that's probably true."

"If he left," she said, suddenly, "he must have taken a horse, right?"

"Right," I agreed. "Smart girl. Come on, we'll check the stable and see if there's a horse missing."

When we got to the stable, Sinclair was there, doing his work, rubbing down one of the horses.

"Sinclair."

He turned and looked at us with his expressionless eyes.

"Yes?"

"Sinclair, are there any horses missing from the stable?"

"Missing?" he asked, frowning.

"Yes, could someone have taken a horse and ridden to town without you knowing about it?"

He thought about it a moment, then said, "It's possible. We have many horses. I would have to look."

"Would you look now, Sinclair, and see if any are missing?"

He paused, then nodded shortly. Diana and I stood by as he walked the length of the stable, checking all of the stalls, and then came back.

"There are five horses missing," he said, "but they are accounted for."

"Have you seen Deke Talon?"

"I do not know the names of the players," he answered, picking up his brush and starting on the horse again.

"Have any of the players taken a horse?"

"No."

"Then the five horses that are missing are accounted for by Two Queens hands?"

"Yes."

"Any buckboards or buggies missing?"

"They would have to be drawn by horses, wouldn't they?" he asked.

"He's got you there," Diana muttered.

"All right, Sinclair. Thank you."

He nodded and continued brushing the horse.

As we left the stable Diana said, "That means that Talon either walked, or he's hiding around here somewhere."

"I doubt that he walked," I said. "So I guess he's around . . . but where?"

"The only way we're going to find out is to look," she suggested.

"We're just as much strangers here as he is," I said. "How would he know where to hide, and how would we know where to look?"

"Well," she said, "I guess maybe that means somebody's hiding him, so I guess someone is going to have to help us look."

"How'd you get so smart?" I asked.

She smiled and said, "I've been learning a lot since I hooked up with you."

TWENTY-NINE

"I'll instruct Rollo to help you," Tyson said, "although I can't imagine where the man could be hiding."

"We can't either, Mr. Tyson," I said, "which is precisely why we need someone who knows the area. . . . But Rollo . . ."

"Rollo is fairly new here, but he knows this neck of the woods very well. He's made a point of learning all about it."

"But if we should have to ride—"

"In spite of his size, Mr. Adams, Rollo is actually a very good rider. He has a special saddle, and Sinclair assists him on and off the horse. I really can't think of anyone else to give you. Joseph knows very little beyond the house itself, and Sinclair has his work—"

"That's all right, Mr. Tyson, we'll take Rollo . . . If he'll agree."

"He will do what I tell him. Go out to the barn and tell Sinclair to saddle your horse and Rollo's." He looked at Diana and said, "Miss Caine, would

143

you care to stay and have lunch with me."

"If you don't mind, Mr. Tyson, I'll go with Cl—with Mr. Adams and Rollo. I could use the ride."

"Very well," he said, taking her rejection very well. "Rollo will be along shortly."

"Thank you."

"Not at all," he insisted. "What you are doing will benefit us all. I for one would like this nightmare to be over. . . . Do you think the others will still play?"

"They'll play," I replied. "We'll see you tonight for the game."

He executed a short bow for Diana's sake, and she and I left and walked back to the stable.

"He's an odd man," she commented.

"I've noticed. He changes character like a chameleon. One minute he's in perfect command, and the next he's confused, and even afraid. . . ."

"Which is the real Tyson, I wonder?" she said.

"I wonder. . . ."

When we reached the stable I relayed Tyson's instructions to big Sinclair, telling him to saddle two horses, Rollo's and one for Diana. I also told him that I would saddle my own.

"Beautiful animal," he said, and went off to get the other horses. Diana stayed with me and watched as I saddled Duke.

"God, he's big," she said.

"Who?" I asked, throwing my saddle on Duke's back. "Sinclair, or Duke?"

"Both of them. I wonder how Sinclair would look on Duke's back."

"He wouldn't be there very long before he'd end up on his own back," I said, "or on his head. Come

on, let's go, Duke. We're going for a ride, big
fella."

"He looks like he understands you," she said.

"He does," I said. "We understand each other
better than most people do."

"We understand each other pretty well, don't we,
Clint?" she asked, coyly.

"I did say better than *most* people," I reminded
her.

When we got outside Sinclair was nowhere to be
found, but there were the two horses all saddled
and ready to go: the bay mare that Diana had used
twice before and a dappled gray with a funny-look-
ing saddle. The only way I could describe it is that
if I were to ride the dappled gray, my knees would
be next to my ears.

"Where's Rollo?" Diana wondered aloud.

"Receiving his instructions, I guess."

"Where do you think he'll take us?"

"I don't know. There must be a line shack somewhere that Talon could be hiding in, or a cave in
the mountains."

"What will we do once we find him?"

"Turn him over to the sheriff," I said, "at least
for questioning."

"That seems to bother you."

"I don't know," I said. "My memory about Talon
hasn't come back, but I don't get that kind of a
feeling about him."

"What kind of feeling?"

"That Talon was somebody that I arrested or anything like that," I explained. "I don't know—"

"Here come Rollo and Sinclair," she said.

What an odd couple they made walking from the

house to the stable area. As big as Sinclair was, Rollo was walking faster than he was, always a couple of steps ahead.

"Let's get going," the little man said as he reached us. "Sinclair!"

The big man bent over and picked up the smaller man in his hands as easily as if Rollo were a child— and it would have been child's play for Sinclair to crush the small man in his hands. Instead, he very gingerly lifted him and placed him in the saddle of the dappled gray.

"Are you ready?" Rollo demanded of us.

We exchanged glances, and then I said, "We're ready, Rollo." We proceeded to mount up—Diana doing so without assistance—and I said, "Lead on."

We spent approximately three hours in our search, and when darkness began to threaten, we turned back.

Rollo spoke very little during those three hours. He simply showed the way and we followed. He took us to a line shack, a couple of valleys, a cave, and a few other places—ravines, old deserted ranches—but we came up empty every time, never even saw a sign that Talon had been in any of those places.

"It's getting dark," Rollo said, unnecessarily. "Do you want to turn back?"

"Yes," I said. "We've got to get some rest before the game."

"You really think there's going to be a game tonight, huh?" Rollo asked.

"There'll be a game," I assured him.

He shook his head, chuckling evily and was about

to make another remark when he was torn from his saddle by a shot. It was as if someone had roped him and yanked him off the horse, and he hit the ground with a thud.

"Get down!" I shouted to Diana, but it wasn't necessary. She had already leaped from her horse, and seeing that she didn't need me to get her out of harm's way, I jumped from mine and told Duke, "Go!" I didn't want to take the chance of a stray shot hitting him. I knew that he'd trot off and wait at a reasonable distance.

I hit the ground and drew my gun while I rolled for cover. There was a second shot, and then it was quiet.

"Diana!"

"I'm all right. What about Rollo?"

I was crouching behind a rock, and from where I was I could see the little man lying on his side. I thought I detected some movement from him, but I couldn't be sure.

"Rollo!" I called. When there was no answer I called his name louder, and this time I definitely saw him move, although he didn't answer me.

"Rollo's alive," I called to Diana.

"Did you see where the shot came from?" she asked.

"No," I said, looking around now to see if I could locate the source. It was almost dark, though, and I couldn't see much—but maybe he couldn't either.

"Diana, can you hear me?" I called to her, but in a lower voice.

"Yes!"

Good. She was able to hear me, and I was reasonably sure that the shooter couldn't.

"I'm going to make a run for Rollo and carry him to cover," I said. "If he fires, see if you can locate the muzzle flash."

"All right."

I holstered my gun, because I wasn't going to do any shooting. I was going to try and grab Rollo on the run and carry him to safety, and I was hoping he wasn't heavier than he looked.

"Okay," I said, getting ready. "Now!"

I ran out into the open and the shots began to come immediately. Whoever was doing the shooting was able to squeeze the shots off quickly, but I tried to put the flying lead out of my mind.

I ran in a crouch, and when I reached Rollo I slipped one hand behind his knees and the other behind his back and lifted him. He was heavy, but I was able to handle him, and I kept running, looking for some cover. We were at the base of a hill, and the rifleman was obviously at the top, shooting down at us. It's hard to shoot accurately when you're firing downhill, and I was hoping that he'd hit Rollo just by sheer luck.

I reached the cover of some large rocks and ducked behind them with Rollo. Just as I was crouching down, a bullet ricocheted off one of the rocks. After that I was out of sight, and the shooting stopped.

"How is he?" Diana shouted. We were further away now, and there was no way we were going to be able to communicate without the gunman up the hill hearing us.

"Rollo," I said, rolling him over.

"Shit," he said from between clenched teeth. His eyes were shut tightly against the pain, and he was still doubled over. I was afraid he might have had

a belly wound, but when I examined him I found
that he'd been hit on the left side. I took the neck-
erchief that he had tied around his neck and pushed
it inside his shirt, against the wound.

"See if you can hold this tight," I told him. His
eyes were still shut, but he moved his hand and put
it against the wound, stopping the bleeding, I hoped,
or at least slowing it down.

"Clint?"

I didn't answer Diana right away, because we
didn't know whether the rifleman had been shooting
at one of us or at Rollo. If I told her that Rollo was
dead, and the little man was the intended target,
then the rifleman might pack it in and slip away. If
I told her he was still alive, the rifleman might stay
to keep trying.

"Clint, are you all right?" Diana shouted, sounding as she were about to panic.

"I'm fine," I called back.

"What about Rollo?"

I decided to let the guy think he'd killed the little
man.

"He's had it!" I shouted to her.

It was silent, then, and I broke the silence by
asking, "Did you see where the shots came from?"

"Up the hill, in those trees," she said. I looked
up the hill and there was a patch of closely set trees
that would give a rifleman good cover.

I left my gun in my holster, because at that distance it wouldn't be much good. I cursed myself
for not grabbing my rifle as I jumped from Duke's
back, but that wouldn't have helped much, anyway,
because I still couldn't see anything to shoot at.

The only thing we had in our favor was the setting

sun. As soon as darkness had completely fallen, we might be able to slip away, or the rifleman might just give up, not wanting to come any closer. He'd have to expose himself on the hill, and a man who would shoot from ambush is not going to have the courage to expose himself afterward.

"Clint, what are we going to do?" Diana shouted.

I decided to lie to her again.

"As soon as it's fully dark, I'm going to try and get up that hill," I called out to her.

"You can't—"

"The darkness will give me cover," I said, interrupting her. I was shouting even louder than was necessary, now, but I wanted whoever was in those trees to think that I was going to come after him.

"Just sit tight, Diana, and don't talk anymore."

She didn't answer, which was good. It was going to be a battle of nerves now, and an ambusher was always at a disadvantage there.

Sitting up among those trees, not hearing or seeing anything down below, he'd start to imagine all sorts of things. Every noise he heard would be magnified into imminent danger and before long he'd be hearing noises that weren't even there.

Of course, the same could have been said for us, but my experience wouldn't allow that to happen to me. I just hoped that Diana's nerves would be good enough.

"Are we just gonna sit here?" Rollo demanded, tightly.

"That's just what we're going to do, Rollo," I said. "He'll give up pretty soon, and then we can get you back to the ranch, or maybe town, and have you fixed up."

"Town's too far," he said. "It will have to be the ranch."

"Fine, that's where we'll go."

"What about the horses?"

"The horses are nearby," I said, as if I were dead sure of it. Actually, the only thing I was sure of was that Duke was nearby. I was hoping the other two horses would follow him and not scatter; this way when I called him over, they'd follow him back. The last thing we needed was one horse among the three of us, even if one of us was only three and a half feet tall.

"You could leave me here, you know," Rollo said suddenly.

"No," I replied. "I couldn't."

I could see him shaking his head and under his breath he said, "Dumb," and I let the remark pass.

He was probably right.

Five minutes went by, then ten, and then twenty. After a half an hour it was pitch dark, with a quarter moon. Night vision allowed me to see part way up the hill, but even the clump of trees was now invisible.

"Why'd you tell the girl that I'm dead?" Rollo said.

"Just in case you were the target," I said. "If he thinks that he was successful, he'll leave."

"What if he wasn't shooting at me?"

"He's going to get nervous and leave, anyway," I said. "In fact, he's probably gone already."

"Christ, then let's get out of here. This hurts like the devil, and I'm losing blood."

"Let me check, first," I told him.

I peered over the rocks we were hiding behind,

then took a deep breath and stood up.

Nothing. No shots.

I walked slowly out into the open, standing there like a sitting duck, but still there were no shots.

"I'll be right back," I told him. "I'm going for the horses."

"I'm not going anywhere," he replied, and I grinned to myself. The little man had guts, that was for sure.

I started walking to where I thought Diana was, and called to her softly so she wouldn't be frightened. As it turned out, it was a good thing I did call, because she had taken a derringer from her boot and might have put a slug in me if I hadn't.

"What are you doing with that?" I asked when I was alongside her.

"I keep it for protection against snakes," she said. "Especially the two-legged kind."

"Well, point it somewhere else," I said, pushing it aside. She looked at it as if she hadn't realized she'd been pointing it at me, then lowered it and said, "I'm sorry. Do you think he's gone?"

"I'm almost positive," I said, "but stay under cover until I get the horses."

"They're probably long gone."

"The other two might have stayed with Duke, and he's close by."

"I hope so," she said. "I don't relish walking back to the ranch."

"Sit tight," I said. "I'll be right back."

"Right."

As it turned out, Duke's leadership qualities had triumphed over the other horses' natural fears, and they were nearby with him, as I had hoped. I grabbed all three reins and walked them back to where Diana was.

"Come with me," I told her. We walked to Rollo with the horses between us and the direction of the shots. I kept Duke on the inside next to me, so he'd be safe also. It wasn't fair to the other animals, but then they hadn't been with me for years looking out for my welfare.

When we reached Rollo I asked him, "Do you think you can ride?"

"What kind of a dumb question is that?" he demanded. "Of course I can't ride."

"All right," I said. "You'll ride with me."

"You going to carry me?" he asked, not sounding pleased with the thought.

"You got a better idea?"

"No," he grumbled.

"Then I suggest we get the hell out of here."

THIRTY

I carried Rollo along with me, while Diana led his horse behind her bay mare. When we got to the house we turned Rollo over to Sinclair, who carried the little man to his room, and Tyson sent one of his hands into town for the doctor.

"The others are waiting," he told Diana and me.

"To play?" Diana asked.

Tyson nodded.

"Even after what happened out there?" Diana asked, turning to face me.

"There is not much you can do for Rollo," Tyson said, "and the doctor will be here soon."

Diana and I exchanged glances while Tyson waited, and then I nodded and said, "Give us a half an hour to clean up, will you?"

"We'll wait for you," Tyson said. "Without Talon there are six of us, so we'll play at one table."

"Start four-handed if you want," I said. "I'm sure Monte Blake wouldn't mind."

"We'll wait for you," Tyson said, again, and he went into the other room to tell the others that we were back.

"Clint—" Diana started, but I shook my head at her.

"Upstairs," I said, and she nodded.

We climbed the stairs and I took her arm and turned her towards her room.

When we were in her room with the door shut behind us she said, "Clint, I can't just ignore what happened and sit down to a poker game."

"Good," I told her. "Without you in the game, I'll have a better chance of coming out the big winner."

"And I'm just supposed to sit up here by myself?"

"With the door locked."

"No, thanks!" she said. "I'll play, but I need a bath."

"I have to clean up, too," I said. "I'll meet you back here in twenty minutes."

She didn't like the idea of being alone, but she said, "All right."

"Keep that derringer of yours handy, near the tub."

"I will," she said. "Hurry back. . . . And be careful."

"I will."

I left her room and waited until I heard the lock click before I walked to mine. I entered my room very carefully and relaxed when I found it empty.

I stripped down, keeping my gun close at hand, and cleaned up using the pitcher and basin. I didn't want to take the time to bathe in the tub; I wanted to get back to Diana as soon as possible.

I dressed in fresh clothes, strapped on my gunbelt, then removed the .22 Colt New Line from my saddlebag and stuck it in my belt, inside my shirt.

The little gun had saved my hide more than once since the time I took it off a dead man, and it might just do it a few more times before we parted company.

Comfortably armed, I left my room and went back to Diana's. When I knocked on the door she called out for me to wait a moment, and a few seconds later I heard the lock click open.

"Come in," she called.

I opened the door and stepped in, and she was standing in the center of the room, soaking wet, with a towel wrapped around her.

"You didn't ask who it was," I scolded her.

"Who else would it be?" she asked, tugging the towel up.

"Try the killer," I suggested, which made her shudder.

"Are you going to get dressed?"

She stared at me and I knew there was something weighing heavily on her mind.

"Clint, we could be dead tomorrow."

"We won't be."

"No," she said. "I'm being realistic. We could be dead. And tonight I want to feel alive."

With that she loosened the towel from around her and let it drop to the floor. Droplets of water stood out on her pale skin, and her nipples were erect.

"Please," she said. "Make me feel alive."

"Diana," I said, wanting her, but knowing that there were people waiting for us downstairs.

"Please, Clint," she said, coming towards me.

So, for the second time that half hour, I got undressed. I picked her up, feeling her flesh damp against mine, and carried her to the bed.

Her passion was intense, fired by desperation. She was single-minded in her attempt to take as much pleasure from the situation as possible, and I did my best to keep up with her.

She slid herself down between my legs and took me into her mouth, caressing me with her hands at the same time. She began to suck on me, and when she felt me swell, threatening to explode, she released me, climbed up and impaled herself on me forcefully. We climaxed together, quickly and fiercely.

"My God," she said afterward. "I've never been . . . like that. It was so . . . so violent."

"It was something, all right," I agreed. I held her and stroked her hair, trying to soothe her.

"I'm sorry," she said, not looking at me. "It was like I was using you for my own purposes."

"That's all right," I said, tipping her chin up and turning her face my way. "I was here to be used, Diana."

"Still, it wasn't right," she said. "I had no right to demand this of you."

"I know," I replied. "You really twisted my arm, didn't you?"

"I didn't give you much of a choice."

"We always have our own choice," I told her. I touched her shoulder and said, "There will be other times, Diana."

"I hope so," she said, then she took a deep breath and let it out as a long sigh. "I guess we'd better get dressed, huh? We've probably got some pretty irate poker players waiting for us."

Yeah, I thought, *and one killer.*

THIRTY-ONE

"It's about time!" Monte Blake called out as we entered the room together. "What the hell were you doing—"

"Never mind," Barnaby spoke up. "Let's just get this over with."

"Talon never showed up, eh?" I asked, holding Diana's chair and then taking my own place.

"Not a sign," Pop Walen said. "You find anything?"

"Just somebody to shoot at us."

"Has the doctor arrived to look after Rollo, Mr. Tyson?" Diana asked, showing genuine concern over the little man's condition.

"Not yet," Tyson replied. "But Joseph is very capable, and he is caring for him until the doctor does arrive."

"Was he hurt badly?"

"It doesn't appear to be too serious a wound," Tyson answered, "but he did lose a lot of blood."

"He'll be all right," I said.

"Let's play cards," Blake said, picking up the deck. He dealt out six cards, face up, and the high card was a queen, landing in front of Diana.

"The lady deals," Blake said, gathering in the cards and handing her the deck.

"Five-card stud," she announced, and the game was on.

There's an old chestnut that I never put any credence in, and that is that it's unlucky to win the first hand of a poker game. I'll take any hand I can get—first, last, or any in the middle. I had no choice in the matter of the first hand that night, though. My mind was out at the base of that hill, wondering who the real target was, but somehow the hand just fell in my lap.

By the time the five cards were dealt, I had a ten, jack, queen and king showing, and an ace in the hole, for the straight. Blake had a pair showing, and the way he was betting I was sure he was sitting on two pair or three of a kind. Barnaby and Diana had dropped out, and Pop looked like he had a pair of aces, with one on top and one in the hole. Aces are usually good in five-card stud.

Usually.

Blake had a pair of Kings showing and the bet was his.

"Fifty."

Pop Walen called—as I said, a pair of aces is usually good, and he was trapped into staying.

"Up a hundred," I said, throwing the money in, and Blake examined me across the table.

"Walen's got aces, Adams," he said, "which gives you two chances to make that high straight. Barnaby folded nines, and Miss Caine folded a nine, which gives you one chance that way. The odds are against you."

"I raised a hundred, Blake," I said. "The play is to you."

He grinned and said, "I play the odds, Adams. That's why I'm a winner." He counted out his money and said, "I raise two hundred and fifty."

Suddenly, aces didn't look so good anymore, and Pop Walen folded his hand.

"I raise the same amount," I said, throwing five hundred dollars into the pot. My mind may not have been totally on the game, but I knew an ace-high straight when I saw one, and who knew when I'd see another one.

Shaking his head, Blake said, "You're bluffing, and I'm going to raise you a thousand."

"You put a lot of faith in two pair, Blake," I said, counting out my money. "I call you thousand, and raise you another," I said, which put me right at the end of my stake.

"All right, Mr. Gunsmith," Blake said. "I'll call." Instead of waiting for me to show my hand, he turned over his hole card, revealing that he had three kings.

I caught his eyes and held them as I turned over my hole card, and he refused to look away.

"Ace," Barnaby said, with no surprise in his voice, but Blake looked surprised.

"What?" he demanded, looking away from me and fastening his eyes on my ace.

"Sorry, Blake," I said. I pushed my cards aside and raked in my pot. Blake stared as his money crossed to my side of the table, and the look in his eyes was ugly.

"Come on," he snapped. "Who deals?"

The deal passed to Pop Walen, who was seated

on my right, between me and Diana. Barnaby was to my immediate left, with Blake on his left, across the table from me. Pop picked up the cards, shuffled, called, "Seven-card-stud," and dealt.

It went pretty much the same way for the first two hours of the game. I was making incredible buys, even to the point of beating Pop Walen's four jacks with my own four kings, and the whole time Diana was looking at me. I knew what was going through her mind. Without even trying, I was on my way to being the big winner of the night, making me next on the killer's list.

I winked at her, shuffled the cards, called draw and dealt.

As had happened so many times during the first two hours, Blake and I bumped heads that hand, only this time he came out on top, holding a flush to my three of a kind.

Laughing, he raked in his pot, and suddenly the luck had swung his way. He was hot for about an hour, and the combination of my hot streak, his, and an increase in the amount of the betting wiped Pop Walen out first.

"That's it, people," he said, shrugging. "I'm out. I think I'll turn in, Mr. Tyson, so I can get a headstart early in the morning."

I wasn't sure whether or not to let him go upstairs. If he wasn't the killer, he'd be vulnerable. Sure, he wasn't the big winner, but the killer could always change his style. The other side of the coin was, what if he was the killer? Yet, I couldn't see the old man strangling those stronger, younger men with a length of cord.

Tyson looked at me, as if asking me if it was all

right, and I answered for him.

"Okay, Pop. Get a good's night sleep. Better luck next time."

"That's an optimistic thought," he said.

"For better luck?" Diana asked.

"No," Pop said. "That at my age there'll be a next time. Good night, all."

"'Night, Pop," I said.

Across the table, Blake was holding the deck, watching Pop walk out, and I said, "All right, Mr. Blake. Deal."

THIRTY-TWO

After another hour, during which play was pretty even, we took a break, and I found myself standing at the bar with Barnaby.

"I heard you had some excitement," he commented. "Figure out who the target was yet?"

I shook my head and said, "No, although I don't know why anyone would want to kill Rollo. My feeling is that it must have been me he was shooting at."

"He?"

"Whoever was doing the shooting," I said. "I have to figure it was a man. The only woman involved in this whole thing is Diana, and she was with us."

"What about—" he started, then stopped short.

"What about who?" I prompted.

He grinned and said, "The cook—what's her name?"

"I assume that's a joke," I said, but before he could reply, Tyson approached us.

"Shall we play cards, gentlemen?"

Tyson had left the room during the break, so I asked him if the doctor had seen Rollo.

"The doctor has been here and gone," he told me. "He bandaged Rollo's side and recommended that he stay in bed for a few days."

As far as I was concerned, that just about finished Rollo as a suspect—unless, of course, the shot meant for me hit him by accident, and the rifleman had actually been working with him.

Every time I thought I eliminated somebody, they pushed their way back in—except for Pop Walen.

And Diana Caine.

So who was the killer? Blake, Barnaby or Tyson? And if it was Tyson, was Sinclair his weapon?

"Let's play cards," I said, and we went back to the table.

I got hot again, for about an hour, and then it switched to Diana, and that worried me. I didn't like the idea of her being high on the killer's list. I started playing to try and beat her, and as a result I started to beat myself. I'd try and bluff her out of a hand, and I'd end up losing too much of my own money. I decided to settle back and wait for the streak to come back around to me.

I had a long wait. Diana cooled off, and it went across the table from her to Barnaby, who had been playing it close to the vest up until then.

Up to that point, Tyson was the only one who hadn't gotten hot, but he had enough money so that he was still in the game.

After Barnaby had taken a pretty big pot, Tyson looked at his pocket watch and said, "It will be daylight soon."

"So?" Blake demanded. "You want to go to bed so some killer can slip into the room and strangle you?"

Everybody looked at Blake, and he continued. "So far somebody's been killed every night for three nights, so why give him a shot at number four?" he demanded. "Let's just keep on going and get this over with so we can get out of here."

"I hate to say this," Barnaby said, "but I agree with Blake. If we don't go to bed, he can't kill someone tonight."

"What about Pop Walen?" Diana asked.

"If we are assuming that the killer is one of the players," I said, "who's going to kill Pop? We're all here."

"How about Deke Talon?" Barnaby asked.

I hadn't forgotten about Deke Talon; it was just that I still had a hard time thinking of him as a killer.

"Are we gonna talk or play?" Blake demanded.

We exchanged glances around the table; there were a few curt nods, and then I said, "Deal 'em, Blake."

This put a crimp in my plan, but there was a chance it might work out for the best. Besides, I wasn't the big winner yet, and to quit there and then would also have ruined my plan.

A thought struck me then, and I wondered what the killer would have done if he had been the big winner one of the past three nights. Kill whoever was second to him?

Or maybe he just made sure he wasn't the big winner. Obviously, winning wasn't what he was after; money was obviously not a motive for him at all—the dead men's winnings had all been intact. He was out to kill some or all of the players, and

I was wondering what we all could have had in common. I knew I had never played with any of these people before, but some of them had played with others. As far as I could tell, though, this exact group had never been assembled at one game before this week, so what else could we have all had in common that would mark us for a killer? At that point I became aware that Blake was talking to me.

"It's your bet, Adams," he said. "If you want to sleep, then throw your cash in and go ahead."

The cards were dealt for seven-card stud. I had a ten on the table, and two more in the hole, so instead of throwing all of my cash in as he suggested, I simply bet a thousand.

"A thousand?" Blake asked.

"Why not?" I replied, grinning at him. "We don't have any secrets from each other, do we?"

Everyone called, because if you don't play you can't win. The cards went around again, and Blake ended up with a pair of queens. He was high man on the table, and in spite of the fact that I had made such a large initial bet, he threw five hundred into the pot.

"If you've got three tens, friend, you'll raise," he said, confidently.

"I raise a thousand," I said.

He shook his head and said, "You're bluffing this time," but he didn't raise, just called.

When we had three cards on the table, Tyson and Diana dropped out, which left Barnaby, Blake and me. Blake still had those queens, and Barnaby had three hearts.

Grudgingly, Blake checked to me, and I bet five hundred.

"Raise five hundred," Barnaby said, and Blake looked at him in surprise, and then down at the three hearts. One of Blake's queens was a heart, and the ten I had on the table was a heart.

"You're bucking the odds, Barnaby," Blake said. "Too many hearts around."

If I remembered correctly, Diana had folded with a heart. I couldn't recall whether Tyson had had one or not, but that accounted for six of them, which left Barnaby with a possible two out of seven chance to pull his flush.

Unless he already had it, that is.

"I call," Blake said, and dealt out the sixth card. He dropped the three of hearts on me and hit Barnaby with an eight of diamonds. He dealt himself a matching card, and he now had two pair on the table, queens and eights.

"A thousand," he said, without hesitation.

I studied Barnaby, because he was the one I was worried about. His face revealed nothing though, so I called Blake's bet and waited to see what Barnaby would do.

"Raise five hundred," he said.

He was playing it coy. By raising five hundred instead of a thousand, he could have been trying to sucker us in, make us think he wasn't all that strong.

It worked with Blake. The look on his face said he thought he had it made, and he raised it another thousand. When I called, Barnaby raised him a thousand, and Blake gawked.

"You only raised five hundred before," he said in an accusatory tone.

"Now I'm raising a thousand," Barnaby said quietly. Blake grunted and called. When I called, he dealt us our last card, down.

There's a unwritten rule in poker: Play it like you have it, even if you don't. Blake knew the rule as well as anyone did, so he immediately bet a thousand dollars. There was too much money in the pot now to play around. Nobody was going to go out, no matter what the bet was.

"I raise two thousand," I said, throwing three thousand dollars into the pot.

"Make it five," Barnaby said, and he threw in five thousand, raising me two.

Blake was uncertain, breaking the unwritten rule, and now I knew that he had no better than two pair. He would probably have liked to go out, but he couldn't be sure I'd call Barnaby's raise, and he wanted to see Barnaby's cards.

He threw four thousand dollars into the pot, calling both raises with a scowl.

Barnaby looked at me expectantly, and as he had probably figured I would, I raised him again.

There was already better than thirty thousand dollars in the pot, and I said, "Raise twenty-five hundred."

Blake let the air out of his lungs in a disgusted sigh as Barnaby called, and stared at the ceiling.

"Five thousand to you, Blake," I said.

He gave me a cold look and turned his cards over, folding without a word.

I turned over my hole cards, showing the two tens and the other three, which combined with my open cards to give me a full house.

"Beats my flush," Barnaby said, and I raked in the pot.

From the looks of it, Blake was almost finished,

sitting with no more than a couple of thousand in front of him. Diana was still in the game, but Tyson looked like he too was in trouble, unless he intended on using more than what was sitting in front of him.

I had about sixty thousand in front of me, which meant that if I had dropped that hand, I would have been in just as much trouble as Blake. Even though he'd dropped the hand, Barnaby looked like he had as much as I had, and maybe more. He hadn't been the big winner on any of the other nights, but he had won consistently, building his stake up little by little. Another couple of hands could have finished Blake, and a little after that, Tyson could have been out, which would leave the three of us: Barnaby, Diana and me.

What would the killer do if we finished out the game today, I wondered, and there was only one winner? Would he kill that one person and let the rest go? Or would he still try and kill us all?

The deal passed to Diana, and she shuffled the cards and then started to deal them out for a hand of five-card stud. Daylight had come a while back, but no one was paying any attention to the time. We all sensed that the game was winding down much earlier than any of us had thought it would when we had started, but the death of three people— which also took their money out of the game and put it in Sheriff Fulton's safe—had speeded things up.

"It's your bet, Clint," Diana said quietly. I looked down and was surprised to see the ace of spades sitting in front of me.

The card of death.

Thanks.

THIRTY-THREE

An hour later, Monte Blake was out of the game and not very happy about it.

"What a waste!" he snapped, standing up with a scowl. "How could anyone concentrate on poker with everything that's been going on around here?"

"If you do this for a living," Barnaby said, "you should be able to concentrate at all times."

Blake threw Barnaby a murderous glare, then said, "I'm going to get some sleep, and then I'm getting the hell out of here."

He stalked out of the room, and then we all looked at each other around the table.

"I suggest we break this off now," Tyson said. He had come back a bit during the past hour, and it had become obvious that the game would go on longer than we had expected a couple of hours before.

"I agree," Barnaby said, picking his money up off the table. "I don't mind admitting that I'm getting a little groggy."

"All right," I said, nodding to Diana. "Shall we

start later this evening at the regular time?"

"That sounds fine," Tyson agreed, also picking his money up from the table.

"I hope you won't mind if I don't come down for breakfast, Mr. Tyson," Diana said, stifling a yawn.

"Of course not," he said. "I'll tell the cook to make just enough for Mr. Walen and possibly Mr. Talon—if he shows up. I think the rest of us will want to sleep for a few hours. Perhaps lunch?"

"That sounds good to me," I said, and Diana and Barnaby nodded their agreement.

"Could we check on Rollo before we turn in, Mr. Tyson?" I asked.

"I don't see why not," he said.

"If you all don't mind, I'll go right upstairs," Barnaby said. "I'll see you all later."

We all went out into the entry foyer; Barnaby went up the stairs to the second floor, and Diana and I followed Tyson across to the other side, where Rollo's room was.

We followed him down a hall towards the back of the house, where he opened a door and let us into the little man's room.

Joseph was there, standing at Rollo's bedside, apparently also checking on his condition.

"Joseph?" Tyson said.

The manservant looked up and said, "He's sleeping, sir."

I approached the bed, staring intently at the little man. After a few moments I was able to make out the rise and fall of his chest as he breathed.

"He seems to be all right," I said.

"He's sleeping," Diana said. "So now can we go upstairs and do the same?"

"Why not?" I asked. "Mr. Tyson, I think we'll see you a little later on."

"Rest well, Mr. Adams," he said. "I think tonight's session will be the last."

"I hope so," I said. "At least we kept anyone from being killed last night. We broke the killer's string, so now we'll have to see what happens."

Diana tugged on my arm and we left the room and started upstairs. At the head of the stairs she yanked on my arm again, dragging me in the direction of her room. She opened the door and practically pushed me in, and I said, "Impatient, aren't you?"

"Not for your body, if that's what you think," she said. "I'm too tired for that."

Looking disappointed, I said, "For what, then?"

"Who won?" she asked, anxiously.

"Who do you think?"

"I lost track," she said. "I know you were very hot a couple of times, but Barnaby stayed consistent."

"It is either Barnaby or me," I said. "I'm not really sure, but I don't think it really matters all that much right now."

"Why not? You said the killer would try for the big winners."

"But the night is over," I pointed out. "We'll have to wait until tonight's session—"

"But what if we go on all night again?" she asked. "What will the killer do then?"

"He'll get impatient," I said. "That's for sure, but as for what he'll do . . ." I trailed off, shrugging.

"We'll just have to wait and see."

"We haven't discussed the shooting," she said. "Who do you think the target was? Was it Rollo?"

I shook my head, both as an answer and to clear it. Sleep was starting to make some serious demands.

"I think I was the target," I said. "And I'm sorry you were put in danger."

"Oh, shut up," she scolded me. "Come on, get undressed and into bed. You look like you're out on your feet."

"You don't look so good, yourself," I said.

"We could both use some sleep."

We undressed and got into bed together, which brought up some interesting alternatives to sleep, but we both realized just how much we needed to rest.

"Don't take this personally," she said, closing her eyes as her head hit the pillow.

"I just might," I replied, closing my own eyes. "If I could stay awake long enough to make the effort."

THIRTY-FOUR

I woke some hours later with a start, and as sound asleep as she must have been, Diana felt it.

"What's wrong?" she asked.

"Something just occurred to me," I said, pulling back the covers and swinging my legs to the floor.

"What?" she asked, sitting up.

"I've got to find something out," I said, grabbing my clothes and starting to put them on.

"Wait for me," she said, jumping out of bed.

"Why don't you get some more sleep?"

"Because if the killer gets impatient, I don't want to be up here alone," she said. "Give me ten minutes."

I couldn't blame her for that, so I waited while she got dressed, and then we went downstairs.

It was afternoon, and lunch was being set out for whoever wanted it. We found Joseph in the dining room, and I asked him the question that was on my mind.

"Joseph, has the sheriff been here yet?"

"Sir?"

"Hasn't the sheriff been notified about the shooting yesterday?" I asked him.

"Yes, sir."

"But he hasn't been here yet to question Rollo or Miss Caine and myself."

"Not that I know of, sir."

I looked at Diana, and she said, "Is that what you were thinking about?"

"Thank you, Joseph," I said. I took her arm and led her out of the room. In the foyer I said, "Why hasn't Fulton been out here yet?"

"Who knows?"

"I want to find out," I said. "Let's ride into town and ask him."

"I'm with you," she said.

Sinclair wasn't in the livery, so I saddled Duke, and the bay mare for Diana, and we rode to town.

On the way she asked, "Have you placed Deke Talon yet?"

"I've scarcely had time to think about it," I said, "but no, I haven't."

"How much bearing do you think identifying Talon would have on this?" she asked.

I looked over at her, but she was staring straight ahead.

"Why do you ask?"

She shrugged.

"I was just wondering how important Deke Talon's real identity was to finding the killer."

"Diana, what do you mean by 'his real identity'?" I asked. "Are you telling me that you know who Deke Talon really is?"

She took a few moments to answer, and I didn't

push her. I let her make up her own mind.

"All right," she said. "Yes. I know that the man calling himself Deke Talon is really . . . somebody else."

"And why didn't you say something before this?"

"He asked me not to."

"So you knew him before?"

"We had met before," she said. "I didn't know him very well, but I knew he wasn't Deke Talon."

"Who is he, Diana?" I asked.

Now she looked at me, and her eyes were worried.

"Clint, I'm sorry," she said. "I never meant to lie to you—"

"You haven't lied to me, Diana," I said. "You simply didn't tell me that you knew who Talon was. You haven't actually lied to me . . . not yet, anyway."

"Do you remember when I asked you if you thought that the Pinkertons would be brought in?"

I remembered, and said so.

"That was because I recognized Talon," she said. "His real name is Draper, Roy Draper, and he's a Pinkerton. At least, he was when I met him, a couple of years ago."

"Damn," I said, remembering now. "He was when I met him too, only with me it was more than ten years ago. That's why I couldn't remember. He's changed a lot since then." We rode a few moments in silence and then I said, "A Pinkerton. Did he say why he was here?"

"No, he just asked me not to give him away. He said it was very important."

"Did he say that he was still a Pinkerton?"

She thought a moment, then said, "He didn't say that he wasn't."

"Why didn't you give him away, Diana?" I asked. "What was between you two years ago?"

"Nothing...really," she said. "He helped me...stay out of jail. I got mixed up in something I shouldn't have. Draper...got me out. He was working on a case, and he got me out."

"And what did he want in return?"

She smiled ironically and said, "What do you think?"

"And you gave it to him?"

"Yes," she said.

I decided to drop the discussion of what happened two years ago. The only bearing it had on what was happening now was the fact that it had kept Diana from giving up Deke Talon's true identity until now.

"All right," I said. "Assuming Draper/Talon is still a Pinkerton, there could only be one reason a Pinkerton would be here, and that's if they were hired—but hired for what? To do what?"

"He didn't say."

"And where is he? Is he alive or dead? Who was he here to investigate, and did it even have anything to do with the killings?"

"And what about the real Deke Talon?" she asked.

"I don't know," I said. "I'm sure that the real Talon was invited to play; for some reason, he agreed to allow Draper to take his place. Why?"

"I don't know," she said.

And I didn't, either, but I intended to find out. Now that the question of Deke Talon had been resolved in my mind, there was another question that was eating at me.

What had happened to Fulton? Why had he not come out to the house with the doctor, to question us about the shooting?

I was starting to get one of my least favorite feelings in the world. I was starting to smell a bad lawman. . . .

THIRTY-FIVE

We tied Duke and the bay to the hitching rail in front of the Two Queens Hotel.

"Now what?" Diana asked.

"I guess there's nothing to do but go and see Fulton," I said.

"Maybe he couldn't come to the house because he was too busy," she suggested.

"When I was a lawman and somebody got shot, I dropped everything else," I said.

"Well, maybe he's not as good a lawman as you were."

"I've been thinking that very same thing."

She must have sensed something in the way I said that, because she stared at me oddly, with a question in her eyes.

"Let's go over to see if he's in his office," I said.

"You sound as if you don't expect him to be there," she replied.

"Do I?"

"What's going on in your head, Clint?" she asked. "You've been acting funny since you woke up."

"I act funny when I get wind of a bad smell," I told her.

"What bad smell?"

"Fulton."

"I'm confused," she said, shaking her head. "I thought Deke Talon was the bad smell."

"He was, but you cleared that up."

"And now the sheriff smells?"

"Right."

"Just because he didn't come to the house last night to question us about the shooting?"

"That's part of it."

"What's the rest?"

"You'll see."

When we reached the office I knocked on the door, and then opened it. I allowed Diana to enter ahead of me, and then closed the door behind us.

Fulton wasn't there. I started to prowl about the room and Diana asked, "What are you looking for?"

"His safe."

"Are you going to rob him?"

"It's the other way around, I think," I said. There was a door leading to a back room, off the cells, and I opened it and went in.

She followed me in and said, "What do you mean?"

"Diana, go to the front door and watch for Fulton. If you see him coming, let me know."

"What are you going to do?"

"I'm just going to look around," I answered. "Go on."

She walked to the front window and I continued my search for Fulton's safe. It was against the back wall, a small three-foot-square box, and it was wide open. There were a few items inside, but none of the money he had taken from the ranch—the property of the dead men—was there.

I hurried into the front room and Diana said, "It's all clear."

"Let's go," I told her, opening the front door.

"Where?"

"To the bank first," I said, "and then I think we'd better get back to the ranch."

At the bank I asked for the manager. I told him I was one of the guests at Mr. Tyson's house, and Mr. Tyson was interested to learn how much money had been deposited in the bank by the sheriff, which he had confiscated from the house. The manager knew about the murders, but he said that Sheriff Fulton had not deposited any money in the bank.

"Are you sure?" I asked.

"Quite sure, Mr. Adams," he answered. "The sheriff has a small safe in his office. I imagine he's keeping the money there."

"Yes," I said. "I'm sure he is. Thank you."

Outside the bank I said, "Let's get to the horses."

"Am I getting the right idea?" she asked, as we hurried towards the hotel. "That the sheriff is involved, and may even be the murderer?"

"He's involved, all right," I said. "His safe is empty, and he didn't make any deposits in the bank."

"But he took their money," she said. "He said he had to take their money and all their possessions."

"And he did."

"Then where is the money?"

"Wherever he is, I'm sure he has the money with him."

"Then that was his whole plan?" she asked. "To kill the big winner every night, and then confiscate their money?"

"And when he had most of the money, he'd leave town with it."

"But how did he know who the big winner was each night?" she asked. I stared at her and she said, "He had somebody working with him inside the house."

"Yes," I said.

We reached the horses, mounted up and started back to the ranch.

"There's one thing I'm not sure of, though," I said.

"What's that?"

"I'm not sure that Fulton is the killer, or that he even planned the whole thing."

"That would mean that the person inside made the plan and did the killings."

"Right."

"Then who is it?" she asked.

"That I still don't know," I replied. "But I think we'd better get back to the ranch fast. Somehow, I don't think that the sheriff and his partner are going to be satisfied just with the money they've gotten so far." I looked over at her and added, "They're going to want it all!"

THIRTY-SIX

As we approached the ranch we slowed down.

"There's no point in rushing in and advertising our arrival," I said. "Let's see if we can slip around back and leave the horses in the stable without attracting attention."

"All right."

We walked the horses to the back of the house and left them in the stable without taking the time to unsaddle them. Who knew, we might even end up needing them again.

"Now what?" she asked.

"Now we're going to try the back door," I said, "and see if we can get into the house unannounced."

"Am I going to need my derringer?" she asked. "If I am, I'd like to get it out of my boot right now."

"That might be a good idea," I replied. "Why don't you tuck it into your belt, where you can get at it easily if you have to."

"Boy," she said, digging it out and tucking it into her belt, "I bet I'm doing just what a lot of men would like to be doing."

"What's that?"

She put on a very stern face and said, "Standing gun to gun with the famous Gunsmith."

I made a face at her and said, "Let's go, partner."

We approached the back of the house without being seen and when I tried the rear door we found that it was unlocked, so in we walked.

"Let's go quietly," I reminded her. "I have a feeling this is all coming to a head."

She stared at me and nodded, and then touched the derringer in her belt for reassurance.

"Let's go," I said and started down the hallway.

Halfway down the hall she grabbed my elbow. "This door," she said, pointing to a door we had just passed.

"What about it?"

"Isn't it the door to Rollo's room?"

I looked up and down the hall, trying to get my bearings, and then realized that she was right.

"Yes, it is," I said. "Let's look in on the little man and see how he's doing."

She nodded and backed up a few steps. I reached for the doorknob, turned it and entered without knocking, hoping Rollo wouldn't mind.

He didn't. He was dead.

"Oh, My God," Diana said. Rollo was lying in the bed face up and there was a large hole in his chest. His blood had soaked into the sheets all around him.

"I wouldn't have thought he had that much blood in him," I commented.

"Poor little man."

"Yeah," I said. I walked to the bed to take a closer look at the body. He'd been shot once through the chest and he must not have been expecting it, because there was a look of pure surprise on his face.

"Who would want to kill him?" Diana asked, then she grabbed my arm and said, "Clint, do you think this means that he really was the target last night?"

"The more I think about it," I replied, "the more convinced I am that we were all targets—or at least, he and I were."

"Well, I could see why the killer would want you dead," she said. "You're looking for him. But why Rollo?"

"There's only one reason I can think of," I said. "Since he obviously wouldn't have been a victim otherwise, I think his partner just got greedy and wanted him out of the way."

"His partner?" she asked. "You mean he was working with Fulton?"

"That's my guess."

"That would mean that Rollo was the murderer," she said, first staring at me and then at Rollo.

"Look at his hands," I said.

"What about them?"

"Look at the size of them, and his upper arms. I'd say that for his size, Rollo was a pretty powerful man. I don't think it would have been very hard for him to sneak into any of the dead men's rooms and wrap a piece of cord around their necks while they were asleep."

"Rollo?" she asked, still not able to accept it.

"Well, when we find Fulton, we can find out for sure," I told her. "Come on."

We left the room and closed the door behind us.

We continued on down the hall until we got to the foyer.

"Stay here."

"Alone?"

"I want you to cover me with that little derringer of yours," I said.

"Well, if you put it that way..."

She took out the derringer and looked at me.

"Well, go ahead."

"Don't get bossy," I said, chucking her under the chin, and then I moved out into the hall.

I wanted to get to the other side, to look in the dining room and the poker room. The house was too quiet, and I wanted to find out where everyone was.

The first person I located was, unfortunately, Sheriff Fulton.

He was behind me.

"Adams," he called. I stopped, because I seemed to recall leaving Diana behind me to cover me. That meant that Fulton had to be behind her.

Which meant that he had me covered, which wasn't what I had in mind at all.

"Fulton?" I asked.

"That's right," he said. "I've got your girlfriend and her little gun, Adams, so if I was you I'd do like I tell you."

"What do you have in mind?"

"Keep your hands away from your body until I tell you different," he said. "I know how fast you are with that gun."

"You flatter me," I said, sticking my arms away from my body at shoulder level.

"Now with the left one reach behind your back

and take your gun out of your holster, then drop it on the ground."

"I could pull a muscle doing that."

"Do it!" he snapped, and I heard a sharp intake of breath which I assumed came from Diana.

"All right," I said. It was awkward, but I was able to reach across my back and grab the butt of my gun, which I dropped onto the floor.

"Very good," Fulton said. "Now kick it away from you." When I did that he said, "Turn around."

When I turned I saw him holding Diana with one hand and his .45 with the other. I couldn't see Diana's derringer, but I assumed it was in his pocket.

He must have come down the hall behind us and jumped Diana when he got the chance.

"What now, Sheriff?" I asked. "Are you going to kill all of us? Or have you already killed everyone else in the house?"

"Just my friend Rollo, so far," he said. "I haven't gotten around to the others yet."

"What's the story here, Fulton?" I asked. "Was it your plan, or Rollo's."

"I can't take the credit for the beginning," he said. "It was originally the little man's idea, and he came to me with it."

"How did it go?"

"Rollo came to me and said that he knew Tyson from way back. He said that his name wasn't really Tyson and that he was wanted by the law under his real name."

"Which was what?"

"He never told me."

"So what did he want you to do? Arrest him without knowing his name?"

"No. The little man had a plan, but he needed me to make it work. He said that he could blackmail his way into Tyson's employ."

"Wait a minute," I said. "He knew about the game, right?"

"Yes."

"And it was his plan to make it look like someone was killing the players, after which you would come in and officially remove the bodies, and their belongings—including their money."

"That's right," he said. "That gun is not the only thing you're quick with, is it?" He pushed Diana ahead of him, and then said, "Let's all go into the dining room."

"Where are the others?" I asked.

"They're all right, for now," Fulton answered.

"But that's not going to last, is it?" I asked. "You can't leave any of us around to identify you, can you?"

"I said you were smart," he commented. "Are you going to go into the dining room?"

"What for?" I asked. "What difference does it make what room I die in?"

"You know," he said, "Rollo was really mad about me hitting him when I was aiming for you." He extended his gun out in front of him, pointing it at me, and said, "I don't think I could miss from here."

"You mean, I was the target?" I asked. "The only target?"

"You were last night," he said. "It wasn't until Rollo started badmouthing me from that bed that I realized I didn't need him anymore. The plan was dead, so I decided to go after the rest of the money my own way."

"Fulton, lawmen like you make me sick," I said, and I knew the disgust I felt was plain on my face.

"Oh, don't give me that bull, Adams," he said. "If you were such a hotshot lawman, you'd still be wearing a badge."

"I have my own reasons for giving up my badge, Fulton," I said. "But you sold yours."

"And at a good price, too. Now, are we going into the dining room with the others?"

"You can blow my head off here, Fulton, and then go and take care of the others."

He frowned, then cocked the hammer on his gun. After a few seconds, he eased the hammer down.

"You're going to do it my way, Adams," he said then. He raised his voice and shouted, "Sinclair!"

Now I frowned and turned in the direction of the dining room. Sinclair had appeared in the doorway and was standing there waiting.

"Either you walk into the dining room, Adams, or my friend here is going to help you."

"Sinclair," I said. "Have you been part of this all along?"

"I made him a good offer," Fulton said.

"Rollo's share?"

"A good enough share," Fulton said.

"You got rid of one partner and took on another?" I asked. Then I realized what he had actually done. "Oh, I see. You got rid of the brains and now you're supposed to be the brains, huh?"

"Sinclair—" he said.

"Rollo was a bigger man than either of you," I

told them. "You were both intimidated by him."

"I ain't intimid—I ain't that at all," Fulton said. "I just didn't need him anymore."

"Sinclair," I said. "You let Rollo bother you, even though you could have crushed him in your hands anytime you wanted to. Now you're going to let Fulton control you. Take control of yourself, damn it."

"Sinclair, help Mr. Adams into the other room," Fulton said.

"Sinclair—" I started, but the big man was moving towards me, and it was time for action, not talk. I set my feet and waited for him to reach me.

The closer he got, the bigger he seemed to get, and just as I had accused him of being intimidated by Rollo—and now Fulton—I was guilty of the same thing. Not only did he intimidate me with his size, but I allowed it to affect my judgment.

I intended to make a move when he got within arm's reach—*my* arm's reach. I forgot that his arms were much longer than mine, and he reached me much sooner than I'd anticipated. I was on my back before I knew it, looking up, wondering what the hell had happened. My jaw ached, so I assumed he'd hit me. I knew I couldn't give him a chance to hit me again, so I rolled away from him and staggered to my feet.

"Clint!" Diana cried out, but Fulton grabbed her arm again and pulled her back.

The others came out of the dining room to watch. Tyson, Barnaby, Pop Walen, Monte Blake and Joseph. Next to Joseph stood a small, elderly woman I took to be the cook.

So he hadn't killed anyone but Rollo—yet.

Sinclair moved in on me again, and he moved well for a big man. Still, I felt I had the edge in speed, and maybe in intelligence, but if I ever let him get those arms around me, I'd be finished.

"Sinclair, this isn't right," I said, backing off.

"Save your breath, Adams," Fulton said. "You told him to stand up for himself. Well, I've offered him enough money so that he can afford to do just that, and he's not going to let you take it away from him."

Sinclair's face was emotionless as he closed in on me. From the look there, I couldn't tell whether he was planning to simply move me into the dining room, or kill me. By all rights, I should have assumed the latter, but somehow I didn't think the big man would do it, not the way he was with horses.

"Sinclair, listen—" I said, but he cut me off by moving in on me fast. I ducked aside and stuck out a foot, trying to trip him up, but he had good balance and kept his feet. He turned and started coming for me again.

I feinted to my left, and when he moved to cut me off I threw a hard right hand into his face. My fist bounced off as if his head was made of solid bone, and he didn't even have to shake it off. It had no effect on him whatsoever. Behind me, Fulton laughed shortly.

"You're gonna need more than that, Adams."

He was right. What I needed was a two-by-four or a gun. A two-by-four I would have used, but a gun...I didn't want to have to kill Sinclair, and I wouldn't unless it became absolutely unavoidable.

I feinted left again, but he showed himself to be

smarter than I thought he was and didn't go for it. When I swung my right he blocked it, then swung his own. I pulled my head back to try and avoid it, but even though his fist only glanced off my jaw it propelled me backward so fast I had to windmill my arms to keep my balance. I would have succeeded too, if Fulton hadn't stuck out his foot for me to trip over. I went sprawling to the ground, an easy mark for Sinclair, but he didn't take advantage of it as he should have.

"Come on," Fulton yelled. "Come on, take him!"

Sinclair began moving towards me, but he was moving slowly enough to give me time to get back to my feet.

His heart wasn't in what he was doing, and I figured that could work to my advantage.

As he shambled towards me I did something I thought would surprise him. I ran straight for him, and he was caught off guard and actually stopped. I leaped as I approached him and put one foot against his chest. Pushing off as hard as I could, I flew backwards away from him, but he was moved back as well, off balance. I tried to get my balance back before he could. Righting myself, I once again charged him, but this time I set my shoulder and went at him lower. My shoulder struck his belly, and it felt like I was running into a brick wall. I moved him again, but not enough to do me any good. I had brought myself within the circle of his arms, and he reacted.

He had me.

I straightened up, trying to get away, but his arms closed around me. His right hand gripped his left wrist, and his fist pressed into my lower back. He

lifted me off my feet and began to exert pressure.
The blood began to pound in my ears and spots
were appearing before my eyes. I was barely able
to breath, but if Sinclair tightened his grip any further, he'd be able to cut that off. I'd be dead in a
matter of moments.

If he really wanted to kill me.

Fulton must have realized this, because he approached us and began to shout at Sinclair, "Tighter,
damn it, tight! Finish him, you big jackass!"

"Sinclair," I managed to say. "Don't let him turn
you into a killer."

"Do it, damn it, do it, you big dummy!"

Suddenly, the pressure was gone and I was on
the floor, choking as I tried to get my wind back.
Fulton was part way across the room, on the floor.
He'd lost his hat, and his mouth was bleeding, but
he still had his gun. I tried to move my right hand,
but my arm wouldn't respond just yet.

"Get back," Fulton told Sinclair, who was moving in on him. "Get back, damn it!"

I tried to call out to Sinclair to stop, but my voice
wasn't working either. I watched helplessly as Fulton pointed his gun at Sinclair and fired once. The
big man's body jerked at the impact of the bullet,
and Sinclair's body jerked with every hit, until the
fourth. At that point he stopped moving and seemed
to teeter on the brink of collapse. He turned to face
me, standing between me and Fulton, and as the
blood began to cascade from his mouth, he started
to fall.

"Fulton!" a voice shouted at that point, and
everybody in the room looked around to see where
it was coming from. At the head of the stairs stood

Deke Talon—or Roy Draper—holding a gun in his hand. "Put up that gun, Fulton."

Fulton did not hesitate at all. He swung his gun around and fired at Draper, who fired a split second later. The Pinkerton man's bullet plowed a furrow into the floor, but Fulton's bullet struck its target. A hole appeared in Draper's face, and the blood blossomed from it. The gun fell from his nerveless fingers, and he tumbled down the steps like a sack of potatoes.

Fulton watched Draper as his body struck the floor at the base of the steps, and then he started to get to his feet. At that point I was able to move my hands. I got to my knees and unbuttoned my shirt so I could get to the Colt New Line tucked inside. I probably could have used the gun on Sinclair at any time, but had chosen not to. I had no compunction about using it on Fulton however.

Fulton turned his glance on me as I was digging into my shirt for the gun, and it didn't take a genius to figure out what I was reaching for. Under normal circumstances I could have had that gun out before he blinked his eyes, but my arms had been inside the circle of Sinclair's grip, so they weren't functioning one hundred per cent yet.

Fulton had the edge of having his gun out already, but he had dropped it to his side while he was watching Draper's body tumble down the steps. As he realized what I was doing, his eyes widened and he started to bring the gun to bear on me.

I fumbled the gun out, popping a button on my shirt, and cocked the hammer a split second before Fulton did. As I fired I heard Diana scream, and then Fulton's gun went off.

My bullet entered his body just below his chin, and the shot he fired was simply a reflex action. The angle of my shot caused the bullet to exit through the top of his head, and he was dead before he hit the floor.

Epilogue

"So Rollo was behind it all the time?" Tyson asked later.

"That's right, Mr. Tyson," I said. "And he bought—and I do mean *bought*—Fulton into it. He figured that a town sheriff would have a legitimate reason for taking the money out of the house, and no one would argue."

We were in the dining room, and all of the bodies had been removed. Tyson had called for his foreman and temporarily appointed the man as a deputy, since Fulton had never had one. Deputized, the man had gotten some hands to help him dump the bodies of Rollo, Sinclair, Draper/Talon and Fulton into a wagon and had taken them back to town.

Now we were seated around the table, all of us. Barnaby, Blake, Pop Walen, Diana, Tyson and me. Off to one side Joseph stood ready; the cook, Mrs. Bell, was in her room, recovering from all of the excitement.

"Why did Fulton kill Rollo?"

"Greed. He thought he could control Sinclair the

way Rollo had been controlling him."

I noticed that Tyson was watching me, and he was probably waiting for me to say something about the fact that Tyson wasn't actually his real name. To tell the truth, I didn't see the need for it, and I'd tell him that later on, before leaving.

"What about Talon?" Blake asked. "What the hell was he trying to pull out there?"

"Talon's real name was Roy Draper, and he was a Pinkerton agent," I answered.

"A private detective?" Barnaby asked. "What was he doing here?"

"I don't know that we'll ever know that," I said. "Maybe one of you knows why a private detective might be after you, but to the rest of us that'll just be something else to wonder about."

I looked at all of their faces, and it seemed that all of them found someplace to look other than into my eyes—even Diana.

Which one of them *had* Draper been after? I wondered. The Pinkerton man may not have gotten who he was after, but he'd saved my life, and I was grateful to him for that.

"Who did the killings?" Barnaby asked.

"Rollo," I said. I explained it the same way I had explained it to Diana and they seemed to accept it. Actually, I was about ninety percent sure, myself, but that was another thing we'd never really know about.

"Now, what about the money the sheriff took?" Blake asked. "Where is it?"

"I'd be willing to bet that it's in his saddlebags. His horse is here, isn't it?"

"Joseph," Tyson said. "Would you bring Sheriff

Fulton's saddlebags in, please?"

"Yes, sir."

"Some of that money is mine," Blake said, as we all looked at him. "Well, it is."

"That's money that you lost, Blake," I pointed out. "What's lost is lost." I got up and started to walk out of the room.

"Well, what do you propose we do with the money?" Blake demanded.

"To tell you the truth," I said from the doorway, "I don't really care."

"What about the game?" Barnaby asked.

I wasn't surprised. I had been pretty sure that even after what had happened that day, the people still in the game would want to play it out—even Diana.

I'd had enough poker to last me awhile, though, and I said so.

"I'm going to go upstairs and collect my things, then I'm leaving," I said.

"Sure," Blake snapped, "with your winnings."

"I'll keep my original stake and throw the rest of the money back into the pot. You can split it up the same way you decide to split up the money from Fulton's saddlebags. I don't want any part of it."

I went upstairs and while I was packing there was a knock on the door.

It was Tyson.

"I, uh, suppose I should thank you," he said when I admitted him.

"For what?"

"For not giving away my secret. I'm sure you must know by now that Rollo was blackmailing me."

"That part of it is none of my business, Mr. Tyson," I said. "I'm really not interested—"

"It's really nothing very severe," he went on, probably needing to talk it out. "It's actually very simple. I was married once, to a very demanding woman, and if she found out where I am, it could be very, uh, inconvenient for me."

"You mean she'd demand her share of everything you have, as your wife?"

"Exactly."

"Why not just settle with her?"

He made a face and said, "As well as being demanding, she has an equally demanding father and some very nasty brothers."

I stared at him, wondering if it was possible that he was telling the truth, and that Draper, the Pink, had been hired by his wife or father-in-law to find him.

"I don't know how true all of this is, Mr. Tyson, but I really don't care to spend any more time wondering about it."

"Do you think that Mr. Draper, the Pinkerton, uh, knew who I was? Do you think he was sent to find me?"

Something dawned on me then and I asked him, "Did you keep my telegrams from being sent?"

"Of course not. Why would I?"

That was true. He had no reason to believe any of us were anything but what we appeared to be, so why would he keep any telegrams from going out. That had to have been Draper, then. He must have assumed I'd recognized him and had wanted to keep me from getting any more information. When I didn't approach him, he must have figured I couldn't quite place him in my memory, and I suppose that was fine with him.

"I don't think you have to worry that Draper contacted your wife, Mr. Tyson," I said, although why I should put his mind at ease was something I couldn't quite understand myself. "He must have been after bigger quarry than you."

"Who?"

I shrugged.

"Maybe the sheriff himself, but the name of whoever he was after died with him." I closed my saddlebags and threw them over my shoulder. "Loose ends are a part of life, Mr. Tyson."

"I sincerely hope you're right, Mr. Adams," he said. "As you have seen in the past few days from my reactions to the, uh, dead men, I am quite without physical courage in extreme situations. If my wife and her family were to come here, I'm afraid I would be lost."

"You've still got your hands, Mr. Tyson," I said. "Treat them right, and they'll stand by you."

He looked at me in surprise and then said, "I believe you're right, Mr. Adams. Thank you."

"There's something else you can tell me now, Mr. Tyson," I said.

"Anything."

"Why the hell did you invite me to this game? I'm sure my poker-playing reputation had little to do with it."

"To tell you the truth, Mr. Adams, you were recommended to me."

"By whom?"

"I should tell you first that this year I received a

number of telegrams from people I had invited, declining the invitation. That's not happened before, and I was becoming afraid that perhaps my game was losing its attraction. To try to remedy that, I decided to invite some famous, even notorious gambler. I decided to invite Wild Bill Hickok—who, alas, declined—and then Wyatt Earp, who also declined. I found it odd that each man suggested that I invite you, as I wasn't aware of your reputation as a poker player. I decided to send you an invitation and was very pleased when you accepted. I was afraid that, as in the case of Mr. Hickok and Mr. Earp, other pressing matters would prevent you from coming. As it happens, I suspect that I am very lucky that you did."

"You asked me here simply to bolster the interest in your game?"

"I'm afraid so—although you did do quite well for yourself. Your friends apparently knew what they were doing when they suggested you to me. Perhaps you would like to play again next—"

"Not a chance, Mr. Tyson," I said, interrupting him forcefully, "not a chance."

We went downstairs together and he said goodbye at the base of the steps, where Diana was waiting for me.

"I have to stay—" she began, but I cut her off.

"You don't have to explain anything to me, Diana," I said. "You're a gambler."

"You make it sound dirty."

It was, as far as I was concerned, in light of what had happened that week, but I didn't tell her that.

"You do what you have to do."

She looked back at the poker room, where I could hear them still arguing, and said, "There's still a big score in there."

"I know," I said, "and you're not going to win it out here."

She kissed me, and then turned to run back to the room, to get them to stop arguing long enough for her to have a shot at her Big Score.